NOTHING MOVED.
NOTHING LIVED HERE.

As they moved deeper into the vast yard, a silence descended upon them. Even Stoor was quiet as they each, privately, took in the horrible tableau. It was an unending gallery, filled with mazelike corridors of the grotesque, the unspeakable. A montage still life of end-moments for men and their machines.

If one believed in them, the place could be aswarm with ghosts. The eidolons of a million soldiers crowding into the open spaces, all drifting in the stoop-shouldered half step of forgotten tramps; as though condemned to shamble aimlessly through the ruins forever.

It was the ultimate metaphor. The final image. The lasting monument to man's need to study war once more....

Fawcett Popular Library Books
by Thomas F. Monteleone:

☐ GUARDIAN   04682 $2.25

☐ NIGHT THINGS   04624 $2.25

Buy them at your local bookstore or use this handy coupon for ordering.

COLUMBIA BOOK SERVICE, CBS Publications
32275 Mally Road, P.O. Box FB, Madison Heights, MI 48071

Please send me the books I have checked above. Orders for less than 5 books
must include 75¢ for the first book and 25¢ for each additional book to cover
postage and handling. Orders for 5 books or more postage is FREE. Send check
or money order only. Allow 3–4 weeks for delivery.

Cost $_____   Name _____

Sales tax*_____   Address _____

Postage_____   City _____

Total $_____   State_____ Zip _____

*The government requires us to collect sales tax in all states except AK, DE,
MT, NH and OR.

Prices and availability subject to change without notice.   8999

GUARDIAN

Thomas F. Monteleone

FAWCETT POPULAR LIBRARY • NEW YORK

GUARDIAN

This book contains the complete text of the original hardcover edition.

Published by Fawcett Popular Library, a unit of CBS Publications, the Consumer Publishing Division of CBS Inc., by arrangement with Doubleday and Company, Inc.

ISBN: 0-445-04682-1

Printed in the United States of America

First Fawcett Popular Library printing: October 1981

10   9   8   7   6   5   4   3   2   1

This is for ROGER ZELAZNY,
Creator of worlds.

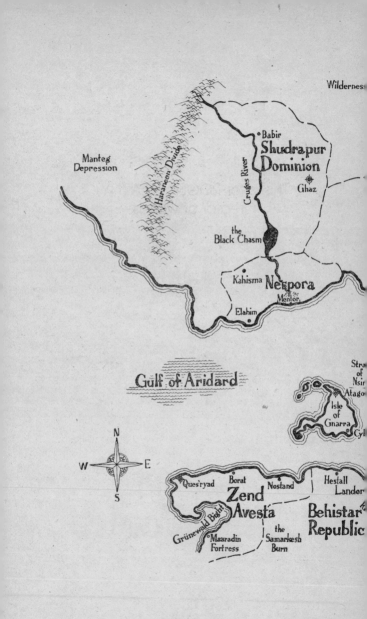

the **Slagland**

Scorpinnian Empire

◈ Calinthia

Vaisya

Kirchou River

Cairn River

◈ Hok

Pindar

Eyck

◈ Prend

Elban River

Mogun

Talthek

Odo

Sanda

Voluspa

◈ Guns
of Kell

Asir

G'Rdellia

G'Rdellian Sea

◈ Eleusynnia

Hester River

the Ironfields

Baadghizi Vale

▢ the Citadel

the
World

It can also be found in the very ancient murmurings of the ancients of even the First Age that there was a bird-thing called the Feeniks. It was a creature which was immortal—dying in a burst of flame, then rising up from its own ashes to live again. So say the writings of Garon and Deldayna of Cairn; it also appears as an analog to the prophecies of Narin, who told of the rebirth of the killer of the Riken. Perhaps the world still waits for that mighty one's return....

—MONOLOGUES OF POULE VI

Yet it is still difficult to accept that the Earth once flowered like the thickest forest of the Scorpinnian, even into the regions of the Manteg Depression. There were men walking the Earth in those days who were different from ourselves. If you ask how this can be, I can only say that they were different in spirit rather than the flesh, but how it can be so, I sadly do not know. As my proof I have only the testament of their machines and the still unturned stones of their once great cities. It is true that we find none of their bones and there are colleagues of mine who say that any bones would have long ago turned to dust. But I disagree.

I fear that they have gone, those great men, to another place. I fear that they have left this world, cleaning up their mess behind them, sealing off any entry to their world, wherever it might now be. For if they were as wise and powerful as I imagine, they most likely saw our "rise" to civilization, and vowed that we would never follow them.

—MANNEN'S *The Perversion*

There is an aspect of death which suggests the infinite, the never-ending, because there will always be death, and Death. The reality of the former, the concept of the latter. And, since there is much now to suggest a never-ending cycle of existence, the world must depend upon death as the catalyst, the prime mover, to ensure a continuation of the cycle.

Thus are we not concerned with the deaths of men—who are by nature insubstantial and generally contemptible—but with the deaths of ideas. For it is the ideas which live and give breath to the future generations, the future eons.

Concern, sadly, is not enough, and the wars continue. The unrest and the petty scratchings of men for power and control continue to poison the earth. It is like a foulness which stains so deeply, spreads so relentlessly, that there is no preventing it. As long as there are men—and it seems that that is part of the curse, i.e., there always will be—there will be the terrible fighting, the maiming death, and purging fires.

—FRAGMENT OF A FIRST AGE MANUSCRIPT
The Great Library at Voluspa

PROLOGUE

There has been a recent period of peace in the World. The temptation exists to say there has also been prosperity, but this would be a falsification of a harsher reality. As in most times, only a small and privileged group *ever* prospers, and this particular time is no different from any other in that regard. It is even a "bending" of the facts to say this is a time of peace because of the continual engagements of the loosely formed countries of Pindar and Eyck.

But the combatants are thankfully small and operate on the easternmost fringes of the civilized World. To the east of the borders lies the Baadghizi Vale, an enormous cawl between the Grayrange Mountains, in which a giant forest of thick, black trunks and thorns like spearpoints flourishes. It is such an impenetrable maze that no man, or fool, ever attempts to pass through it, although it is said that strange creatures have evolved within its confines, having learned to navigate the bolestrangled land and to brachiate daringly across the tops of the great forest.

And so it is possible that Pindar and Eyck shall never be at peace. The claims of rightful borders are always a delicate subject, especially among nations who have a not-very-tenacious grasp of their true self-image. Such is the pitiful state of Pindar, and of Eyck. Neither possesses a governmental system that is much removed from what one might call "musical assassinations." In fact, one of the perennial political jokes in G'Rdellia, a neighboring country of some culture, asks the question: Who's running Pindar *this* week?

And since the only viable exports of these two nations may rightfully be termed unrest, hate, and distrust, it is easy to ignore them when considering the general state of the World. Pindar and Eyck are thus the clubfooted stepchildren of a world that is only marginally more fortunate but chooses not to recognize that basic truth.

It is a world of gross ignorance, galloping pestilence, petty injustice, unrelieved famine, early death, and meaningless existence. It is a world in which the spirit of humankind—that sometimes brilliant, sometimes infamous, driving force that fuels civilization's furnace—has departed. And perhaps the most dismal testament is that the departure has been a slow and ugly thing. It did not leave in a flaming burst of glorious war, but rather it slouched away during the long nights of ignorance and fear. It did this thing so slowly, so insidiously, that no one—or practically no one—even noticed it was missing. Until, of course, it was too late.

But this is not to say that the World is dying, for it is certainly not. More precisely, one might observe that the World survives in spite of itself, and will continue to survive.

And there are the bright spots, the untarnished bits and pieces attempting to escape the corrosions of time. There exists a great, capricious body of water. It is as blue as the eyes of a Vaisyan maiden, as fierce and unpredictable as her mother, and as faithless as her father. Storms and calms walk hand in hand across its shimmering surfaces, courting no ship, no country, and wanting no quarter. It is a vast, moody sea misnamed the Gulf of Aridard. It is surely no gulf—having none of the connotations of serenity and placidity which that term may possess—and almost qualifies as a small ocean. It is a surly, waspish mistress to the nations of the World, which huddle like tramps about a bright fire along its broad shores. The Gulf of Aridard: focal point of the World.

Due west of the Gulf is the Sunless Sea—so named because of the cold mist and rolling fog which ever obscures the setting of the sun on its farthest horizon. It is a monstrous ocean with shifting, rolling waves thirty ems high, valleys equally deep, and the grayest, coldest skies west of the Ironfields. Several expeditions from the maritime nations have attempted voyages into and across the Sunless Sea, but none of the great ships have ever returned. Some of the more optimistic ship captains have described their missions as "crossings," but we historians have cautioned against this kind of positive thinking because it presumes the existence of a landmass, a shore, a *something* on the other side of the Sea.

There is no record in the modern era substantiating the presence of *anything* beyond the Sunless Sea.

Legend, folktale, fragments from the First Age, the oral tradition at large: all these sources speak of other landmasses—Continents, as they were called—but the names of such places, the locations, the sizes, and all other authenticating data have been lost or, perhaps, were never known.

Continuing the geography lesson, one may find to the extreme northwest of the Gulf a very large desert area, lying primarily below sea level and set off by a colossal mountain range known as the Haraneen Divide. This great arid expanse is called the Manteg Depression, and it is generally avoided by most of the World. Fierce sand and dust storms stalk the Depression with an almost cyclic frequency. The intensity, the sheer viciousness of the storms are enough, it is said, to strip the flesh from a man's bones with the clean, crisp efficiency that a surgeon's scalpel could never rival. There are levels of radiation in the Manteg Depression which are still surprisingly high, considering the unknown number of years since thermonuclears may have been employed in the region. Some legends say that there are still silos and installations within the Depression, still cradling rusted and/or scorched ICBMs, although, again, such claims are totally unsubstantiated by the record. (It is hoped that the pictographic or, as some insist, *photographic* technique will soon be perfected so that such claims can be proven without reasonable doubt.)

The temperatures in the Manteg Depression may get as high as 50° Centa. The amount of rainfall the area receives is little more than two cees per year.

And yet there is life in the Depression. A nomadic tribe called the Idri roam about its fringes and high elevations. They ride an indigenous animal called the loka which has evolved an outer hide of such thickness and durability that the sandblast of the storms is nothing more than a refreshing shower. It is cautioned, however, that a beast of such physical toughness possesses a disposition to match. The Idri are a foul-smelling, sun-bleached, and leathered lot, who are neither pirates, nor traders, but a band of simple, breeding scavengers who repopulate themselves to continue a basically meaningless existence. But they bother no one and will probably survive in the Manteg long after the rest of man has finally gone away.

There is vegetation in the Manteg that resembles steel chips and shavings; there are mutant *things* that might have been men at some point in their ancestors' dim past; there are crawling things that live beneath the oven-baking sand and come out at night to suck the fluids from anything which might be sleeping or resting upon the gritty desert floor; there are flying things that ride the ever-present thermals.

But there is little else.

On the eastern slopes of the Haraneen Divide lie two nations of disparate personality. To the south, on the northern coast of the Gulf of Aridard, lies the enlightened realm known as Nespora. Not a large country by World standards, it is not small either. Enjoying a moderate climate and a very fertile agricultural river valley, fed by the clean waters of the Cruges River, Nespora is a prosperous place. At the river delta into the Gulf, the city of Mentor flourishes like a well-kept orchid. It is a cosmopolitan port of call for statesmen, traders, sailors, adventurers, educators, and rulers. A majority of the city is given over to the wealthy controllers of finance and World trade, thus forming a vast, complex center upon which the economic stabilities of most of the other nations now hinge. And so Nespora's nation of traders and businessmen have come to provide a built-in national security system for its people. As the focal point and the kingpin for the World's economy, Nespora is almost unequivocally safe from aggression by anyone. They keep no standing army and do not fear rule by anyone; they are the experts in what they do and *no one* wishes to usurp their unique position as clerks to the World. While its other principal cities of Elahim and Kahisma (a fortress-city guarding an ancient pass out of the Divide) are not as large nor as opulent as Mentor, they are nevertheless comfortable, clean, and possessing some of the finer amenities of modern civilization.

North of Nespora, contained in the west by the Cruges River and the Black Chasm, and to the east by a ragtag "empire," toils the no-frills Shudrapur Dominion. Almost as an afterthought left over from the jagged realities of the Haraneen, the terrain of Shudrapur is rugged, unyielding, and full of rock. The land rolls on relentlessly, as if unconcerned with the legions of peasants who yearly plow and plunder it. There seems to be an independence which permeates this nation. It is a feeling that begins in the land itself and spreads out to the populace, which is mostly represented by thousands of small, pastoral villages, each governed by a small, rustic council of elders—men who became wise because they lived long enough, and vice versa. Agriculture is the key to life in Shudrapur, a fact reflected in the low profile of its only two cities,

Ghaz and Babir. Although there is no real politics, or even a strong current of nationalism among the giant, amorphous collection of peasant-citizens, there is a government in the Shudrapur Dominion which is based in the eastern city of Ghaz. The city is large and spread thinly across a floodplain, where the summer rains are an invitation to the flowering of a million buds. Its architecture reflects the national *weltanschauung:* functional, simple, but without the cold severity of a totally ascetic personality. The country's art and music and literature are conservative, at times moralistic, and, in the final analysis, dull; however, it is a respectable country, a responsible country, and not without its unseen wealth. Its unspoken dedication to the land pays off in a great agricultural surplus which is shipped throughout the northern countries as a desirable trade entity. There is no one of culture and taste who does not delight at the flavor of fruit from Dominion orchards, wines from its vineyards, grains from its waving, rolling hills.

Indeed, if there is anything truly negative to be said of the Shudrapur Dominion, then it must be the Black Chasm. It is a wound in the earth that stretches for more than one thousand kays, and plummets jaggedly into its depths more than twenty. Leaning out over its edges, one stares into infinity, the true bottom of the Chasm lost in the hazy mist which huddles near the deepest regions. The walls are scored and sliced as if from a monstrous cutting tool, the natural rock a blend of basalt and granite and lignite. It is an evil-looking place. No one of sane mind and valued life ever enters the Black Chasm, although in past eras there have been stories of explorers who have attempted it. No one knows whatever became of them; more ever returned or exited from the opposite end. Many Shadrapurians believe that if there exists an entrance to Hell on the surface of the earth, then it is surely here.

Prior mention of an empire to the east of the Shudrapur Dominion can be none other than the Scorpinnian Empire. Easily the largest nation of the modern World, the Empire is a vast land of untilled meadows and uncut forests so thick that it is almost impossible for the summer's light to penetrate. There are huge prairies which roll uncontested from the Eban floodplain north and east to the borders at the Kirchou River; and the soil here is rich and black as night. Legend says that once great battles were fought on this land, and it is the millions of corpses that have, over the millennia, made it so fecund. Irony is often high in the most acrid of cases, and so it is with the Scorpinnians: they are not the World's best farmers, and the majority of their marvelous land passes unused from one generation to the other. The same may be said of the immense ore and other precious metal deposits which abound throughout the Empire—iron, bauxite, thorium, uranium, manganese, silver. They are literally everywhere, waiting to be mined, refined, employed. But they are also untouched, save for a few subcontracts arranged by Nespora which litter the "Emperor's" coffers but do little to enrich the country's standard of living. The foreign mining concerns then ship their ores to the World's industrial centers in Nespora, G'Rdellia, and Zend Avesta, where small, crude factories fashion poor replicas of First Age genius. The state of the nation is not, however, a great concern of the general population, which is scattered throughout the vast countryside in small towns and villages and administered to rigidly by a caste system of governors and other ranks of hegemony. There is a quasi-military aspect which blankets the people like a shroud, and imparts a pallor to their lives, adds to the already dreary regimen of their existence. There is little art, practically no music, and rampant illiteracy. They are a plain, ignoble folk whose best virtue can be described as "dependable," but then the same may be said of horses and oxen. In time of war, they serve their virtue best, having been known to march into the face of overwhelming odds, be slaughtered to the last man-

17

jack, and not sully the battle with one creative protest. The principal city is Calinthia which is settled comfortably, like an obese man in an overstuffed chair, in the geographic center of the Empire. From this spot, the Emperor "reigns"—a duty which is largely concerned with hour upon endless hour of courtly foolery and *de rigueur* obsequiousness, parties, alcoholic drinking bouts, and dancing girls, preferably naked. Naturally the second level of advisors, chancellors, and viscounts have maintained close ties with Nespora, using that nation's worthy emissaries to make use of Scorpinnian's natural resources and continue at least a semblance of commerce and stability. While it would be unfair to say the Scorpinnian government is corrupt, a close look at its two chief ports along the Gulf—Mogun and Talthek—would convince the wary observer that this nation is at best running a treadmill to oblivion.

But there are worse places.

To the northeast of the Scorpinnian lies a bleak and singular place. It is called the Slagland. Like a flat, gray-watered ocean, it stretches to the far horizon, continuing perhaps to the edge of the World itself. It is smooth as a sheet of glass, and equally featureless, being composed of vitrified rock and basalt and melted steel. At one time, far in the world's past, it may have been a huge complex of cities and industries, but something happened which caused even the earth itself to boil like oil in a cauldron. Everything melted and ran like lava, staying hot for perhaps a thousand years, until it cooled into a diamond-hard, *totally flat,* unbelievably dead place. It is a cold-steel meadow where nothing moves, where *nothing* lives.

But as one moves south and west of the Slagland, life appears once more, although grudgingly and with little respect for itself; the aforementioned smears of Pindar and Eyck, which lie huddled along the meanders of the Kirchou as it empties into the G'Rdellian Sea.

To the south of that emerald body of water lies a flower in the midst of arid nothingness: the nation of G'Rdellia. Perhaps the oldest continuing country in the modern World, G'Rdellia is proud of its heritage, its history, and primarily its culture. Although the land is as poor as the Scorpinnian is rich, the G'Rdellians coddled and coaxed and worked the land until it produced for them. They are a nation of *workers*. They sing and smile as they work, weaving it into their culture and their tradition. G'Rdellia is a nation of builders, sailors, artists, traders, and thinkers. In their capital, Eleusynnia, beauty flourishes. There is art here; there is music in the streets. Architecture born of a feeling, design from the philosopher's stone, function following the rigors of meditation, all of these things are found in Eleusynnia. The country is involved in World commerce and is probably second only to Nespora in such skills, but it is also concerned with the propagation of culture, of true humanity, and in this it is second to none. The citizens are autodidactic philosophers, and their concepts of form and beauty have permeated their personal interpretations of logic, but this has become no impediment. The G'Rdellians see the World as a naturally logical place, with everything having reasonable cause and effect. They never attempt to go against this natural cosmic flow. And above all this, there is the long-standing heritage of their status as class-one soldiers. The special sect of Kell Warriors are the most dreaded in the World, but they are employed only in defense of their own borders. The G'Rdellians are by nature a peace-loving, nonimperialist people, although it would not be such a terrible thing if all the World were not at least similar to such a country. Here, at last, peradventure, is a time and a place where a little imperialism would not be a bad idea.

South of G'Rdellia lies one of the greatest mysteries of the First Age. The land, untouched by loving hands and minds as in the north, has become arid and dusty and full of a singular gloom. The soil here is changing into sand and the vegetation is becoming wiry and scrawny, if not dying out altogether. It is called the Ironfields and with good cause: it is a gigantic grave-yard of metal things. Relics from uncounted wars, death dealers of past ages, war machines, whose functions have been long-ago forgotten, lie broken, half-buried, and corroding in the unrelenting sun. Time lies heavy in this place, and there is a scent of death, which hovers about the shifting sands like a raven, only waiting for the chance to strike once again. It is the scent associated with machine oil and cordite, with dried blood and decay. It is believed that there was once a great battle here, a gathering of all the world's tribes to a place where the final solution would be hammered out, then etched forever upon the armor and the bleaching bones—a grim, intolerant scrimshaw. Some say it was the end of the First Age which took place in the Ironfields. Some say that it was only the latest in what must be an endless cycle of Armageddons, and that perhaps the First Age is misnamed—that its proper label should be something like "the Previous Age." Who can say? There is no evidence to refute either argument. Or *any* argument for that matter. Evidence lies in the presence of the broken machinery; evidence which dole-fully says: *We were here, and this is how we fought, and this is where we died.* The mysteries survive their deaths and no one now claims to know who it was who came to this place to fight and die.

It is a philosophical question, and like the myriad others which plague men's minds, there are some places better suited to ponder them than others. One such place lies north of the G'Rdellian Sea; it is the little principality of Odo. As the Shudrapur caters to the World's stomach, Nespora to its purse strings, and G'Rdellia to its aesthetic sense, thus does Odo serve the world's intellect. Its principal city of Voluspa is a ven-erated place, said to have been built upon the ruins of seven other great cities, all upon the same spot. It is a cosmopolitan place, studded with churches and mosques and temples, its skyline a forest of spires and minarets, each vying to capture the glint of bright dawns and fading dusks. Every religion, every sect, every "school" of philosophy has flocked to the shores of Voluspa, each establishing a headquarters somewhere within the labyrinthine streets and alleyways. Universities and libraries also crowd for space among the ancient edifices, and the boulevards are filled with the traffic of monks and priests, the corners abounding with prophets and oracles. It is a city—nay, a *country*—filled with learning, with polite argument, deference and, of course cerebral stimulation. There is, at the Great Library at Voluspa, which rests like a giant stone cube upon the cliffs overlooking the Straits of Nsin, the World's greatest collection of original manuscripts, microfiche, newsfax, processor crystals, and other ana, incunabula, and vella. Scholars, pedants, and the simply curious make pilgrimages to the Great Library to ponder the thoughts and secrets of the past ages. Again irony has had a hand in the demographics and the geography of the modern world: Odo, entranced by the pursuits of the mind, happens to be located in a spot where lesser pursuits can also be found. The city of Voluspa overlooks the Straits of Nsin, which is the gateway from the Gulf of Aridard into the G'Rdellian Sea, and northward to the Kirchou River. It is *the* major trade route in the East, and the Straits of Nsin form a strategic point of control along that route. For this reason, Odo, in conjunction with G'Rdellia, has vowed to always keep the Straits free and open to all ships and commerce. Odo keeps a small, but respected, standing army *and* a large armada of wooden ships, all of which are bound to their country's vow. In the past, countless wars have been fought over the control of the Straits, and Odo does not wish it to become another political bargaining chip or a bright and shining spoil for the next would-be dictator-to-the-World.

Not surprisingly, the most expected spawning ground for such a man would be the Behistar Republic. Located due west of the Ironfields, along the southern shores of the Gulf of Aridard, this country is anything *but* a republic. Without a twinge of conscious guilt, historians and statesmen denounce the Behistar. It is a bellicose nation, crammed with fiercely nationalistic automatons. The people are so rigorously programmed that all hint of creativity or originality has long-since fled their culture, which is as cold and devoid of life as midnight in the Manteg. The Behistar has been ruled over the generations by a succession of all-powerful "Lutens," who have a curious demigod status in the culture. The laws of divine succession to the throne still woefully apply here. A generation ago, the rest of the modern World mobilized against the Behistar Republic and after a terrible conflict, which greatly reduced the resources of *everyone,* imposed upon this vile nation what is commonly called The Interdict. It is a codex of rigidly enforced laws which control all trade, exchange, and movement of the Behistar throughout the rest of the World. There is a sanction against the raising of an army, and the leaders of the country are closely watched. Many believe that the Behistarians enjoy waging war simply for its own sake, reveling in the subsequent destruction and suffering. Its capital city of Landor reflects the sad state of this nation: a filth-ridden, black-stoned sprawl; its impoverished inhabitants scuttling rat-like through its narrow, shadowed streets. If there exists the mirror image of Eleusynnia, it is truly Landor. It is a happy accident which isolates the Behistar with natural barriers: the Ironfields to its east, the Gulf to the north, and the Samarkesh Burn to the west, which is the hottest place in the world. Temperatures soar easily above 60° Centa, and there is a total absence of wind. The dunes do not move; grain upon grain lies dead and unshifting for centuries, unless violated by the errant footfalls of some hapless animal who gets lost within its borders. The Burn is the fiercest surface on the face of the earth: a simple, unassailable truth. Few things live there, fewer still attempt to traverse it.

It is not an impossible barrier, however, and its neighbors to the west, in the expansive nation of Zend Avesta, have little fear of the Samarkesh Burn. Located on the westernmost borders of the Aridard Gulf, Zend Avesta is a vigorous, energetic nation of adventurers, traders, pirates, sailors, artists, and inventors. It is said that if technology triumphs in this, our ragtag World, then it will have its beginnings in Zend Avesta. There are those among us who claim the renaissance has already begun: Tales of First Age artifacts being unearthed or reconstructed wind there way around the Gulf, always having their origins in this marvelous country. Tractors running on the methane gas of animal turds, windmills with Teflon gearings, electric generators, and experimental radio. These are but a sampling of the wondrous things of which men from Zend Avesta dream. Although all the country's cities—Nostand, Borat, Ques'ryad, and Maaradin—are exciting, pulsatingly alive cities, there is no equal to the wonder which is Ques'ryad. Alabaster towers, sparkling lakes and spires, courtyards and hedgerows, wide boulevards, aflame with the flags of a hundred thousand families, tribes, and societies. It is a city of movement and life. The merchants' stalls are alive with the languages of the World, the great quays which open upon the Sunless Sea offer sanctuary to the ships of the World. Great wooden vessels, their furled masts a tangle in the westering light, flock to Ques'ryad like moths to the dangerous flame. It is the largest port city on the Gulf, and a haven for traders and pirates, beggars, and kings. It is the jumping-off point for archaeologists, explorers, outfitters, and adventurers. If there is any romance, as well as classic danger, remaining in the World, then it resides in Ques'ryad.

And so one may grasp the confines of the World. Not an overwhelming mass of cultures, but enough to keep the lesser men confused and wary of one another. For as long as there will be differences, as long as men take breath, there will be wariness in the World. In so writing these words, I am reminded of yet one more place which bears mention. It is such an isolated place that one might easily ignore it, forget it. The Isle of Gnarra. Actually a small island group, the remnants of a volcanic caldera, the Isle lies southeast of the center of the Gulf of Aridard. Administered by an age-old monarchy, a family now rife with gene infestation, hemophilia, and congenital idiocy, the people of the island-nation slough away at life as their grandfathers have taught. They are fishermen and shipwrights, shepherds and farmers, and little else. This Isle remains in the backwash of current affairs and is largely ignored by all the powers-that-be, however it is the home of very old religions—now in disfavor or out of metaphysic vogue—and it is said by some yellow-eyed sailors and other wary travelers that the Isle of Gnarra is still the seat of occult phenomena. Although rumored the home of wizards, sorcerers, necromancers, and the like, there is little evidence of their influence anywhere in the World—save in the minds of superstitious men.

In summing up then, the World is simultaneously a small and a large place. Diverse cultures and beliefs huddle cheek to jowl about the shores of the only familiar, negotiable body of water on the planet. Beyond the humble borders of these places, no man knows what lies. It is possible that the World has always been a place of darkness and mystery with torches to light the way being few and far apart. But this writer, this "historian," if I may enjoin myself with such a title, does not believe this.

No. I feel that in every myth, there is a grain of truth. In history, a grain of falsehood. And there is *everything* in between. We cannot know what will yet come, and we may not wish to recognize what has come before, but I believe there are lessons in the buried stones, warnings in the bleaching bones, testaments within the rusting machine hulks, the black skeletons of the aircraft uncovered by wind and shifting sand, or the fused and twisted hulls of gray ships, which the oceans occasionally heave upon our shores.

We cannot turn our backs on our heritage—whatever it may have been. If there are mysteries, and if we are men, then we must solve them.

—*A Short Commentary on the State of the World*
(from the notebooks of Granth of Elahim)

ONE

It did not, at first, seem as if it would be a special day for Varian Hamer. But he was wrong.

Standing on the deck of *The Courtesan,* he watched the last reflecting paths of the morning sun break up and depart the emerald surface of the Aridard Gulf. There was a slight salt breeze, and the sounds of the great docks of Mentor were rising up about him like the communal hum of hive insects as they set about their work.

"All right, you blooders! Get those arms pumping! Let's go!" The first mate stalked the fo'csle, glaring at his crew, warming up his voice for a long morning.

Varian jumped the ratlines on the starboard side and reached the first sail of the mizzen. As he worked to unfurl it, his gaze drifted out over the wharves, where other great Gulf ships were preparing to weigh anchor. Like his father before him, sailing was the only profession Varian knew, although he longed to be versed in other trades. His travels had taken him throughout the World. He knew the streets and alleyways of every major port: Elahim, Vaisya, Talthek, Voluspa, Nostand, Ques'ryad, even Eleusynnia and Landor. He was curious and bright and never seemed to have learned enough of any of the places he'd visited. He always wondered what lay beyond the horizon of the Gulf cities. Surely there was more to the World than the few dozen ports which crouched along the shores of the Aridard.

Varian Hamer was almost two ems tall—large for a man of these times. His dark hair was long, flowing down to his shoulders in curly locks. He was not heroically muscled, but he was not thin. His dark eyes sparkled despite the loss of contrast with his deeply tanned skin, the badge of the Gulf-ship sailor. He was clothed in the traditional brown-and-whites of a merchant seaman, girdled by a thick belt and a shortsword on his left hip. Varian was skilled in the use of weapons, having had the good luck to have sailed on the famous *Nightshade* with a renowned weapons master, when he was barely fifteen years old. The *Nightshade* had been the biggest, fastest merchant ship on the Gulf, and her fabled black-and-gold hull was recognized throughout the World as a beauty and a marvel. She sailed the gulf for almost two generations, untouched by fate, or storm, or Behistar Raiders, until she was purchased by a wealthy bureaucrat in Borat. She was outfitted with a new crew and enough provisions to sink her watermark, and sent out on an expeditionary journey: an attempted crossing of the Sunless Sea.

That was the last seen of that proud and beautiful ship.

Varian had not sailed with her because of his youth and inexperience, but he often wondered what had happened to her crew. One of them had been Reg Furioso, the famous weapons master of Sanda. An old man by the time Varian met him on the *Nightshade,* Furioso was still as keen and hard as his vast panoply of first-quality blades and pistols. During the long lulls in the voyages across the Aridard, Furioso schooled the young Varian in the uses and techniques of the pike, the broadsword, the shortsword, the cutlass, the sidearm (or pistol), and the rifle. At all times, the old man stressed the dominance of the *spirit* over the flesh, having learned his deadly crafts through the ancient masters of Odo, the seat of philosophic understanding in the modern world.

Hence, Varian assimilated a blend of religions, cultures, and philosophies—all pointed to the mastery of killing and maiming, yet filled with marvelous digressions which gave one fascinating ways in which to view the world. And so, by the time Varian had reached his present age of thirty years, he was an expert in all the lethal businesses. There were literally thousands of ways to kill a man, and Varian was familiar with most of them. As with such men, their reputation travels specterlike ahead of them, and there was, then, a period in his life when he was being asked to prove the worth of his reputation.

He did.

And now that period of macho challenge was at an end. Varian's motto could have been "Nobody bothers me!" for it was indeed true.

"You there!" A voice seemed to pierce him like an arrow. "Get down here!"

Varian was yanked from his reminiscences by the voice of the first mate, a thin, sinewy, oily-haired fellow, who was standing directly below.

Dropping down the lines, Varian landed at his feet. "Yes sir?"

"You're Hamer, one of the new men?"

"That's right. Anything wrong, sir?"

"I'll ask the questions, if you don't mind." The first mate eyed him with a look that was neither kindly nor malicious, as one might appraise wares in a vendor's stall.

"Sorry, sir."

"The captain didn't have any papers ready on any of you new men. I just want to get a few things straight in my mind. I like to know my crew, if you know what I mean." The first mate almost grinned, then apparently thought better of it.

"Certainly, sir."

"Good. Now then; last ship?"

"The Dragonfly, out of Asir."

The first mate's expression changed, passing through flashes of surprise, curiosity, and grudging admiration. "That was a bad wreck, I heard. How many men'd she lose?"

"All but ten of us. She carried a crew of eighty-four. Storm came up out of nowhere, caught us as we were leaving the Straits, and we broke up on the rocks."

"Aye, that's what I heard. How'd *you* make it?"

"Luck, I'd guess, sir. And some strong swimming." Varian ventured a smile, hoping that he did not appear cocky.

"Any special skills I should know about?"

Varian considered the question. It was best not to talk about combat skills or knowledge. One was asking for trouble that way since it was often misinterpreted as bragadoccio. He deferred and added only that he was an amateur astronomer and had some basic navigational training.

"That might come in handy. That's good. Stay armed and be alert. There's been talk of some new raiders out of Hestall. We're big enough to tangle with 'em, but you should be aware, all right?"

"Yes, sir."

"We'll be running standard shifts. You'll take your orders from me or the captain and no one else unless one of us designates a lieutenant of the Watch. Clear?"

"Yes, sir."

"All right, Mr. Hamer. Don't forget. You represent the government of Nespora, now. She's a fair and fine country, and her sailors should reflect that image. We treat our sailors fair on *The Courtesan* ...as long as they deserve it. Clear, Mr. Hamer?"

"Yes, sir." Varian was beginning to sound quite repetitive, but he had long experience in dealing with authoritarian types like this first mate. Men such as he have precise, orderly, and simplistic views of the way-things-should-be. Their perception of the world is global and lacking in an awareness of the sheer *com-*

plexity of things. Old Furioso had been quite clear about such men: Speak to them directly, clearly; no big words, no lengthy discourses; obey them as long as their commands are reasonable; but if they get in your way, eliminate them.

The first mate had nodded and was already walking down the deck, searching out other new faces, where he would presumably repeat his little performance and establish his place in the vessel's pecking order. Fine. It was of little importance to Varian. He knew his job, and he did it well. No problems.

The Courtesan would be sailing out of Mentor to Eleusynnia, exchanging cargoes, then back eastward to Ques'ryad for another exchange of cargo, then a brief stop at Elahim before returning to her home port. It was a well-known trade route, called "The Golden Circle Route" because it traveled among the richest Gulf cities in the World and because only the best ships were selected for the trips.

As the morning grew older, the vessel was made ready and prepared to shove off. By this time the docks of Mentor were ablaze with the color and movement for which the "jeweled city" was so famous. Vendors and tradesmen, beggars and kings all walked shoulder to shoulder in the avenues and quays which led to the gangways of ships. Banners thwacked in the sea breeze marking the locations of special booths and stalls; the heralds and colors of myriad royal houses competed with one another for attention and homage. The smells of roasted meats, baked nuts, and pastries rose up and commingled with the dockside smells of freshly netted fish, now cooking in iron brazier pots.

Out of the choreographed confusion, which was the docks of Mentor, came a hunched figure, oddly clothed in the silky brown robes of a monk, complete with hood and roped cincture about the waist. Varian noticed him mainly for his lack of color in an otherwise artist's palette of motion and sound. His assignment done, Varian leaned on the starboard gunwale, watching the hooded person move uneasily through the crowd. Occasionally the figure's face would turn into the sun, and Varian could see that it was an old man, bearded and gray, looking into the crowd's midst, as if looking for someone he knew would not be there.

There was something *odd*, out of place, about the old man, which Varian could not define. That Varian could single him out, a stoop-shouldered beggar, in a molten, viscous throng of color and excitement, was in itself strange. But it was more than that. There was a slowness, a deliberation, with which the man walked among the vendor's stalls and gangways. It was a gait which hinted at great age, older than a man should ever fear to be, as if the man carried the weight of centuries upon those old curved shoulders. And there was a cast to his eyes which also spoke to the ages, as if many generations had unfolded like parchment scrolls before those lonely, almost desperate eyes.

Suddenly, something happened which changed the rhythm of Varian's pulse, caused him to catch his breath. The crowd surged and eddied past the gangways, the old man an insignificant element moving with the flow; but in an instant, his eyes flicked upward to *The Courtesan* and locked in on the gaze of Varian.

It was as though the old man *knew* the sailor had been staring, watching him.

Once the connection was established, it seemed that neither man could break it. Varian thought he perceived a slight nod of the hooded figure's head, then he cut diagonally across the current of the throng, moving deliberately toward the gangway of *The Courtesan*.

What have I done? thought Varian. Grabbed the attention of an old beggar, now to be personally harrassed by him? It was an indignity, an affront to his station and rank. He could not allow his fellow sailors to see such a thing happen to him.

Turning, Varian looked anxiously across the deck, hoping that no one had yet noticed.

"You will listen to me," said a voice.

Varian tensed as a hand touched his shoulder. He whirled defensively, shocked to see the old man beside him.

"How—?"

"I am not as helpless as I appear." Close up, the hooded figure's face appeared to be ageless—not young, not old—simply a man. The eyes were a cold blue, but they reflected wisdom and not a small amount of pain.

"What do you want with me?" Varian took a step backward, unconsciously watching to see if the man made a move toward a possibly concealed weapon.

"I want only to talk to you. That is my...my fate. To talk to people."

"Your fate? What're you talking about? What do you want with me?" Varian did not trust the man.

"My name is Kartaphilos. Have you heard of me?"

The name meant nothing to Varian. He shook his head.

The man laughed softly, nodding. "Always the same. *No one* recognizes the name. But no matter. I've a story to tell."

"Listen, old man, that may be true, but I've a job to do and you're keeping me from it. I would not be a merchant sailor if I had time to sit around and listen to every old gaffer's story. So—"

A hand had grabbed Varian's arm, just below the biceps. It was a young, strong hand. Varian could feel the power and the pressure on his arm, could feel the *reserve* strength which felt as if it could crush his arm to the bone. "But you *will* listen to me, Varian Hamer." The old man's eyes almost glowed.

"How do you know me?"

"I know all the men to whom I choose to tell my story. I'm no crazy beggar! I've watched you. You are a resourceful man, a respected man. Your name is spoken with deference in the bars and taverns around Mentor docks. You were one of the only survivors off

The Dragonfly. She went down in less than a minute. You *know* you were one of the special ones."

An appeal to Varian's ego was never a detriment. "That may be so," he said. "So what do you have to tell me?"

Kartaphilos smiled. "I thought you would understand flattery. It's a universal language, I am told."

"You're funny, but not *that* funny. Don't try my patience, old man." Varian tried to sound harsh, but knew he was not fooling Kartaphilos. The old man had an ineluctable charm about him.

"Very well, Hamer. I will tell you something that I know will pique your curiosity. I know that you are interested in the World, and especially its many mysteries. You are not satisfied with the crumbs of life you receive at the Gulf-port cities. You crave more. You—"

"How can you know such a thing?"

Kartaphilos smiled. "Let's just say that I *know*. Otherwise, it makes the story longer. And you say you have not much time. So let me ask you: Have you ever heard of the *Riken?*"

Varian paused, almost saying no, but trying to recall the name from memory, from some old sailor's tale, from a sea chantey perhaps; he was not sure. A ship's name? No. A ruler's name? Maybe.

"I've heard the name, I'm certain. But I can't place it."

Kartaphilos nodded. "I'm not surprised, on either account. It's a First Age name."

"First Age? Are you sure?" There was something magical, arcane, almost organically attractive about the Ancients. Something dark stirred in Varian's blood.

Kartaphilos nodded again. "Quite sure. At any rate, the Riken—a race of people from the First Age who, some say, were the most ingenious nation to have ever lived in the World. They were not a large country, but their citizens were dedicated to the betterment of the nation to a fanatical degree. Are you sure you have not heard of them?"

Varian shook his head. "No, I think I have...but not much. Lots of superstitious stuff. Some silly legends. They were supposed to be a race of monsters...."

Kartaphilos laughed. "In a way, yes. The Riken were monsters, all right, but not the way you might think. No basilisks or chimeras, just plain men. Men who lost sight of what they really wanted. It seems as if, for some reason, the Riken nation developed a true gift for the sciences. The World's finest mathematicians, metallurgists, chemists, and physicians all received their training in Rikeh. They were men of great knowledge and even greater inventiveness. Forever and a day, the scientists were presenting their government with new wonders, better ways to *do* everything. These men were like magicians, but more mysterious than the sorcerers of Atagoras, more powerful than an Odonian warlock."

"Did they have the power of the birds?" Varian rubbed his jaw pensively, admittedly entranced by the story.

"You mean *flight?*" Kartaphilos laughed. "All of the First Age people could fly! In great machines. Have you never seen some of the wrecks?"

"Wrecks? No, I've heard tales, but I've never seen."

"Too far inland for you. The Manteg Depression. There are some fantastic wrecks in there. Preserved by the climate. Like they flamed-out yesterday."

"I'd love to see one," said Varian absently.

"I'm sure you would. Maybe you will, after you've heard my tale. Anyway, listen closely. The leaders of Rikeh decided to put their scientists' knowledge to the best possible use: domination of others, of course. Expansion into neighboring nations' territories was the first step, then attacks on the entire hemisphere, and finally a global assault. Years passed as the armies and machines of the Riken spread across the lands. Tales grew up of the atrocities and massacres committed in the name of the Riken cause, and most of the stories were later substantiated. Whole cities would be burned out with the heat of a single weapon. Millions of citizens carbonized in an instant. But that was the merciful death. The Riken machine columns and its armies would cut through a city like a shortsword, methodically eliminating *everyone,* using the remains to supply nucleotide vats, agricultural chemicals, food substitutes...."

"What are nucleotide vats?"

"A process which produced living tissue. A form of biology used the vats for purposes which I doubt you would understand." Kartaphilos did not smile.

"How do you know such things?"

"I am an old man. I have traveled much. I listen. I observe. I keep my mouth shut."

"You're running it plenty now."

"I'll stop, if you'd like." Kartaphilos grinned.

"You would not dare."

"No, I would not. Now where was I? Yes, the methodical elimination of enemy populations...It was a dreadful practice which stands unmatched in the history of mankind. There was only one nation in the World which could possibly stop the onslaught of Rikeh—the Republic of Genon."

"Where is Genon? I've never heard—"

The old man gestured with his hand, cutting him off. "It is gone, now. Covered over in the shifting sand of centuries. Even *I* don't know how long ago, or where its exact location had been."

"How long ago? You don't know? How long did the war last?" Varian settled back against the gunwale, reached absently for his pipe and pouch, began stuffing a pinch of bac into the wide bowl.

"How long to make the Slaglands? The Ironfields? I do not know, honestly. No one knows when the First Age truly came to an end, or even *how*. We can only stumble over the broken, twisted pieces of the past...."

"What happened then? Do you know? Genon? Rikeh?" Varian struck a match against weathered wood.

The match flared, a cloud of blue surrounded his head and pipe.

"Genon was a peace-loving republic. No imperialism, free commerce, a thriving technology, the usual bureaucratic corruption, but a basically happy populace with few wants. Naturally, Genon was unwilling to interfere with Rikeh's early territorial skirmishes, but once the thermonukes started, Genon had no choice. The two nations locked horns like stag cragars. Defenses and counterdefenses deadlocked them for uncounted years. Genon instituted the practice of arming each human settlement, village, or city with a *Guardian*. A large central computer with robot servos, anthropomorphic usually, which interfaced with the citizens. It personalized the computer which was entrusted with the welfare of the people. The Guardian machines were equipped with the best defensive systems in the world, and were quite adept at keeping helpless citizens safe from the atrocities of the Riken armies. It was this final tactic which finally broke the back of the Riken, forcing them off their territorial expansions and into a final Ragnarok with the Genonese."

"Ragnarok?"

Kartaphilos shrugged. "You know...the 'Final War'...the 'Armageddon' which fills all the legends. It seems that man is destined to fight these kinds of things indefinitely."

"Yes, I suppose you're right. So go on...."

"There is not much more to tell. The Genonese was the victors, but at a terrible price—the eventual end of First Age dominion over the World. There has been decline ever since. A Pyrrhic victory, it is called."

"What does that mean?"

"Look it up in your history books. Ever go to Voluspa? Yes, of course you do. They have a library there. Visit it sometime instead of a brothel. You might learn something."

"Very amusing, old man. I should—"

"You should listen to me, and pardon an old man for

37

his attempts at humor. The point of all that I have told is quick upon us. Listen. There exists still in the World one last functioning relic of the First Age, of the Last War."

"What?!"

"A Guardian. Still performing its function. Still waiting." Kartaphilos nodded, then looked into Varian's blue eyes.

"That's impossible! Why has it never been found? Where could it possibly be?"

"If something exists, it cannot be impossible. And who really knows what lies within such places as the Black Chasm, the Manteg, or even the Ironfields?"

"Do you *know* the location?" Varian's pipe had gone out; he knocked the burned plug roughly from the bowl, not taking his gaze from Kartaphilos.

"I *did*. At one time, I knew more of the story than I have been able to tell you. It was my...my mission to go out from the Citadel and bring help. I was not to return until I brought the assistance."

"What are you talking about?" Varian felt his heart pounding, felt the growing tightness in his chest. There was no reason why he should believe this old man. But he *did* believe. "What's the 'Citadel?'"

"The place of the Guardian. Don't you see yet? The Guardian *sent* me for assistance. I...I failed it. There was a machine column and Riken support troops. They shot me out of the sky, tracked me. I was...injured, and it took all my skills and few defenses to escape, to re—to heal myself. But afterward, I discovered that something was different. Amnesia, I think it's called. An impairment of the memory, the mind. I could not *remember* everything! For a long time, I could remember nothing, then gradually the pieces of the puzzles began to fall back into place, but never all of them. I did not know where to go to find assistance; I did not know how to go back...."

Varian studied the old man's face. The features were

cracked, seamed with age and fear and sadness. He was telling the truth, this Kartaphilos.

"I believe you," said Varian. "But why are you telling me this?"

"Time has passed and still I remember no more. I have decided that I would never find my way back to Guardian alone. The World is too large. Instead, I have set out across the face of nations, searching out men who are bright enough, curious enough, and strong enough to take up the search."

"You mean I am not the only one you've told?"

"Do not be offended, but no. Hundreds, I'd figure. There were other ways. I could have propped myself up as a prophet or some other type out of Odo, then spent years gathering a crowd of disciples, instilling some religious rigamarole around the facts—a little magic, some fables—and just like that I'd have had a...crusade going. Thousands of pilgrims and believers scouring the lands for the Lost God, or some such rot. But then, I don't think that's what Guardian had in mind when he sent me out for reinforcements...." Kartaphilos smiled weakly.

"But that must have been a *long* time ago! You can't be who you say you are? You can't be that old!"

"But I am."

"The war is over. Everyone's dead. *Long* dead! The Guardian's got to be gone—"

"No!" Kartaphilos screamed the word with such power that Varian was humbled into silence, as if he had spoken a blasphemy. "No, it lives! I *know* it! I feel it!"

Varian smiled. It had been a very convincing tale. The old man was quite an actor, full of detail and nuance, of gesture and just enough information to spring the curious appetite, to allow the imaginative mind to fill in the missing parts. It had almost worked.

"No, old man. You talk foolishness. What you say cannot possibly be."

A look came into the eyes of Kartaphilos which could

be read as anger, or hatred, or perhaps madness. Whatever it was, Varian did not like it. Slowly his hand drifted toward the hilt of his sword.

But the old man did not move toward him. His face twisted into a hideous mask and the voice which now spoke was low and not very human. "It is true. And I shall prove it to you."

"What're you talking about?"

Varian stepped back involuntarily as Kartaphilos reached for the clasp at the neck of his robe. His wrinkled, blue-veined hands grasped at the folds of his cloak and jerkin, ripping them away.

"No..." said Varian, hearing his voice trail off, a weak whisper. "It's not real. It can't be...."

Reaching out, he forced himself to touch the exposed chest of Kartaphilos. The rest of the world went away—the sounds and colors of the Mentor docks—as he focused on the smoked-amber glass of the old man's chest. It was clear and deep as a natural spring, and it danced with the lights of LEDs and microprocessors. Myriad circuits and pathways laced the chest cavity like thousands of roadways in a miniature city. It was a hypnotic display of light, power, magic.

"It's a trick," said Varian, hoping that he was correct.

Kartaphilos shook his head as he let the folds of his clothing drop, covering the body which shone like a precious gem. "No trick," he said, reaching for his neck, pulling up an edge of flesh which had been covered by the robes and hood. It came away easily from the smooth surface of the neck. Kartaphilos began peeling it up, past the neck, stretching it away from the chin and jaw. More amber glass, circuits...

"No!" Varian pulled the hand away. "All right! Not here, please. I believe you." He drew a breath to keep away the dizziness. He felt weak.

With a studied casualness, Kartaphilos tucked the synthetic flesh beneath his robes. "It is not the first time I have resorted to such a demonstration."

"How *old* are you? How could you still be...be working?"

"You have no conception of the skills of the men of the First Age. I am nothing to their science."

"It's so incredible....I don't know what to say."

"You sound more the fool than you are, Varian Hamer. I have shocked you, but you will collect yourself. Say nothing. Only know that you are special. It will take a special man to find the Guardian. Perhaps it is you."

"Stay with me! Help me find your Guardian!" Varian's mind raced ahead. Half-imagined thoughts told him of the power and the wealth which would come to a man who found the Guardian. The secrets of the First Age would lie at the man's feet. The World would be again renewed to its prior greatness...under the direction of that special man.

Kartaphilos shook his head. "No, I cannot stay with you. Just as I can feel it within my body, my pathways, that Guardian still functions—for I would cease to function should Guardian fail—so also can I feel the need for me to continue my mission."

"Why?"

"Because there is no warrant that you will succeed, Varian Hamer. Your bones may lie bleaching in the Manteg while I repeat my story to another young sailor like yourself. It might be said that I am...doomed, or cursed perhaps, to wander the World, telling my tale."

Varian understood what the machine was telling him. "But how will you know if, or when, you ever succeed?"

Kartaphilos shrugged. He was a perfect mimic. "I will know." He straightened himself, eyes glancing to the docks below.

"What's the matter?"

"I will leave you now. There's nothing more to tell. It is up to you now. Either you will search for Guardian or you will not. Either you will find it or you will not."

"Where will you go?"

"I don't know. There are many places I have yet to see. It is still a big enough World. Good-bye, Varian Hamer."

Varian wanted to say more, but his mind seemed to seize up. He was shocked with the knowledge that he would never see the terrifying messenger from the First Age again. "Wait. Please, is there nothing else you can tell me? Where should I begin my search? Any clues? Can't you remember *anything* else?"

Kartaphilos smiled. "There is one last thing. I was saving it for last...."

"What? What is it?"

"Sand."

"What's that? 'Sand?'"

"There was lots of *sand*. I remember that. But nothing more definite."

"That narrows it down a bit," said Varian seriously.

"Does it really? I don't think so. You can be relatively certain that the Citadel resides nowhere within the civilized World, else it would have been discovered by now. Which leaves the more desolate parts—all of which have *sand*."

Something jumped in Varian's heart. Kartaphilos was correct. "Still, it is something."

"Make of it what you can. Good fortune, Varian Hamer. I envy you."

"Me? Why?"

Kartaphilos smiled again. A very human smile. "I envy all of you. You humans. It *must* be a different thing, a marvelous thing to be alive, to be an organic entity. I wish that I could know it."

Varian nodded, understanding. "It *is* a good thing...sometimes."

"Yes, I'm sure it is." Kartaphilos turned and adjusted the cowl of his cloak. "And I leave you, and I wish you success."

Varian could say nothing. He watched as the...thing called Kartaphilos walked slowly to the gangway and shuffled down its incline. His drab clothing was soon lost in the eddying swirls of color in the marketplace. Varian strained to follow his path until it became totally lost in the constantly changing network of the crowd.

Turning his attention back to the ship, he was relieved to see that no one had taken great notice of his conversation. It was not unusual to have visitors upon a ship so grand as *The Courtesan*. If anyone asked, he would tell them that Kartaphilos was an eccentric old uncle, bearing a personal family message. It would suffice. No one who knew Varian Hamer ever questioned his word.

The ship would be weighing anchor soon, and Varian now viewed the voyage in a different light. So much to think about. So much to do. He would now be forced to plan his life as he had never planned it before.

Eleusynnia. Their first port of call—would it be a good place to jump ship? To begin the search? Maps. He would need maps and charts. He must study everything. There could be no snap decisions in something like this. He would go to Eleusynnia at least. From there, perhaps into Voluspa to consult the ancient texts at the Great Library. There might have been a germ of truth in Kartaphilos' suggestion. A careful eye, a careful mind, might find something of use in the old writings.

Something burst into life deep in his being. He could feel it, but he did not yet recognize it. It was something more than the mere joy of being alive. It was the first spark of *purpose* in his life that had ever truly meant something to him.

The sun was burning brightly in the sky now. It was a brassy disk eating through the haze. Somewhere its light burned down on a place of sand...and other things.

And I shall find it, he thought.

TWO

Despite her present situation, Tessa was a woman of character and determination, of intellect and ingenuity. It was both her blessing and her misfortune to be an attractive woman, and there were few men who had not appreciatively eyed her reddish-auburn hair, her green cat's-eyes, her fair complexion. Her legs were long, muscled like a dancer's, but by no means masculine. She was lean but well-proportioned in a way which men desired.

Men. Desire.

Although Tessa was not yet twenty-five, she knew enough of both. As she lay in her cramped bunk of the tradeship, she thought back over the times which had cursed her.

It had been her father who first initiated her, falling prey to the feelings which had stabbed most of the village men, even when Tessa was no more than thirteen years. She could not help her early maturity, or the way her clothes refused to conceal the ripeness, the fullness of her young body. The innocence of childhood had been a merciful veil, but she still felt ashamed when she recalled those early years.

She had been fifteen when the mother had died, and it was raining the day the family buried her on the high hillside, where her father's sheep grazed. The rain washed away everyone's tears, but never the memories.

It was late that evening, after all the other children had been sent to sleep. It was understood that Tessa, being the oldest child, would assume the duties of the mother, although Tessa did not realize how completely her father had decided the change of roles would be.

As she stood tending the cooking fires in the iron stove, banking them and adding an extra log for warmth during the night, her father came and stood close behind her. Even as he touched her shoulder and bent to kiss her slender neck, she knew what he wanted.

His hands were rough, calloused, clumsy. His breath smelled of stale bac and garlic, his body greasy and heavy with the odor of his sheep. Turning, she saw the burning in his eyes, the slight trembling in his hands and his voice as he told her how beautiful she looked, how much she resembled her mother. He mumbled something about how a man's need did not die with his wife as he pressed his large sweating belly against her. Edging away from the hot iron of the stove, she moved to the wall where her father's hands fell upon her, touching her, exploring her with an urgency that was terrifying. It was as though he had been waiting only for his wife to die so that this moment would be at hand.

He would not look her in the eye as he forced her down to the divan, pausing only to turn down a kerosene lamp. Then he was upon her, sweating and heaving, taking her in the darkness. She was so sickened that she could not scream; she could not even cry.

For ten years he abused her until he became stricken with a disease which slowly sapped him of his strength and his ability to walk. The slow paralysis heralded an end to her abuse, but not the degradation. Deprived of his profession, unable to herd his flocks, the father became a businessman. A wealthy trader from the city of Prend offered her father a small fortune—enough to support him for the rest of his wretched life—in exchange for Tessa. Although the merchant dealt primarily in spices and herbs, there was a thriving, though underground, trade in servants and concubines.

The bargain was struck and Tessa was taken aboard *The Silver Girl,* which would follow the Kirchou into the G'Rdellian Sea, with stops in Eleusynnia and Voluspa before putting in at Talthek, where the demand for Scorpinnian concubines brought the World's highest prices—sums which made the amount paid to Tessa's father meaningless. It was a civilized World...only when it chose to be.

And so she sailed now, with a cabin of other unfortunate young women, to the southern end of the G'Rdellian Sea. She knew the government of Eleusynnia would take issue with slave trading, and that she would be safe if she could jump ship once *The Silver Girl* put in at that magnificent city. Tessa had reached the point in her life—which up until now had been a long and featureless repetition of events—where she must begin to live for herself, or finally die. Life as it had been previously mapped out for her was simply not worth the living. She would take chances, she told herself, as she lay in the darkness listening to the sails flap in the night breezes, the groan of the wooden decks, and the occasional grunted commands of the ship's crew.

She spoke to no one of her plans, not even her fellow prisoners, of whom she found none worthy of trust. Most of them were worse than she, a shepherd's daughter. Street whores, orphans, and beggars to the last. Tessa listened to them carp and laugh among themselves, picking up their uneducated accents, trying to place their origins. One was obviously from a settlement north along the Cairn River. Another from the gutters of Hok in Pindar. Still others from the backward provinces near Baadghizi. They all eyed her with, at first, suspicion and, later, hostility because she did not join in their coarse amusements.

There was also the problem of the crew. Hardened

47

men with few pleasures available during the long cruises, they were more than agreeable at the prospect of cargoing a cabinful of future concubines. As each watch changed there were wholesale invasions and impromptu parties, and endless indignities.

By the time *The Silver Girl* reached Eleusynnia, Tessa did not care whether she lived or died. The only thing she knew was that she would not be sailing any farther. She hated her father and she hated the other women and she wanted to kill the men, *all* of the men. They were animals—panting, sweating, stinking animals—who did not speak to her, hardly looked at her, when they hung over her on their elbows and knees. She *hated* them.

But that evening, as the watch changed, there were fewer crew coming to invade them because the ship had made port, and those on liberty would be slinking into the night streets of the city looking for new conquests. This would be one of her best chances, and she moved quickly, selecting one of the smaller men who came loudly into the cabin. He was an older man with small bones and pinched features, a bald head and eyes that seemed to have a trace of kindness remaining.

She drank with the man and let his bony fingers probe and caress her. She forced herself to hold him, to nuzzle into his neck, to laugh at his attempts at bawdy humor. When he was sufficiently full of wine, she begged him to take her up on deck where she might look upon the majestic lights of Eleusynnia under a quartering moon. The man looked at her oddly, but perhaps he was a bit of a romantic himself, for he nodded his head and laughed as he guided her not too roughly from the stuffy cabin.

Tessa had never killed a man before. It was especially difficult because this one had been as close to kind as anyone she had ever accompanied. As he held her against the gunwale, pressing his thin lips against her, she let her hands drift sensually down the small of his back, touching his belt, feeling the hilt of his

48

knife in her long fingers. The weapon felt hard and smooth; she knew she must move quickly, efficiently.

Twisting her body into his, she gasped loudly as she pulled the knife free from its scabbard, immediately plunging it between the lower ribs of his back. The man tensed, then screamed as she tore the blade through him. Something dark bubbled from his lips and his eyes became glassy, unseeing. There was noise and the clatter of boots on the deck, growing louder. Tessa looked from the crumpled shape at her feet to the approaching figures on the deck, then finally to the shimmering oily surface of the water as it slapped lazily against the hull.

Over the side without thinking, she felt a rush of air and a bracing sting of something far colder than she imagined. Her clothes gathered in the water and weighed her down, causing her to struggle as if in a quagmire. Paddling in half panic away from the ship, she heard the rough voices of the men as they searched for her in the darkness, and suddenly a flare arced gracefully out over the harbor, guiding her way to the nearest wharf and exposing her position to the nightwatch of *The Silver Girl*.

Their firearms started popping and cracking, snitting into the water around her. Once she tried sinking, holding her breath and feigning a hit, but when she was forced finally to the surface, the volley of shots began again. Davits creaked in the distance and she heard a boat being lowered. If she did not reach the wharf, they would overtake her and death would be graciously hers. It seemed unfair, now that she had come so close to freedom, to fail.

The wooden pilings seemed to grow closer, but she could not be sure of this. The flare had died out and another was arcing high above her, casting a horrid orange glow on everything. The longboat had smacked into the water and she could hear the angry shouts of the men as they leaned into the oars.

Then there was a hand grabbing her arm. It was a

strong hand which held her like a gentle vise. With a fluid movement, she was being pulled from the water, gliding like a ballet dancer, up and over the edge of the wharf. A tall man with sandy hair and bright blue eyes—they were obviously so, despite the odd illumination of the flares—and dressed in the uniform of a merchant seaman. As he lifted her to her feet with his left hand, he raised a long-barreled pistol in the other.

"Be quiet," he said. "And get down."

Moving away from the edge of the dock, Tessa watched the man calmly take aim upon the approaching boat and open fire. The man in the bow arced out of the boat, his forehead blown away. The rest of the crew drew weapons and began firing wildly. Turning, the man grabbed her arm again, firmly yet gently as before, and ran off down the docks toward the closest avenue. They turned a corner and rushed toward the lights of a tavern.

Before they could reach it, however, the remaining trio from the longboat rounded the corner. Her rescuer pushed her into a doorway and turned to face them, firing off another round from his large sidearm.

A second crewman fell, the one with the small-caliber pistol. Before the remaining pair could move, the merchant seaman broke into a run, hurling himself in between them. He dropped his sidearm in favor of his shortsword, which he unsheathed so smoothly and quickly that the two men did not have time to react to it.

Two quick flashes of the blade were all that were required. Varian stood for a moment between the fallen men, ensuring that neither needed further service from his weapon, then turned back to the doorway where Tessa huddled.

"We've got to leave this street," he said. "Come."

They hugged the shadows of a parallel avenue, and Tessa noticed that the man moved with a confidence which suggested intimate familiarity with the narrow alleys and shaded streets.

50

After three blocks, he stopped her. "You're still soaking wet. You have a change of clothes?"

Tessa could only shake her head.

The man smiled. "All right then; if you'll come with me, I have a friend who might be able to help us."

An hour later, Tessa was sitting by a warm fireplace, dressed in the clean dry robes of a woman named Alcesa. She was very fat and freckled; her blue eyes were pinched into the folds of her face. She walked with an incredibly light touch about the room, attending to Tessa as if she were a returning daughter and seemed to sincerely care about her welfare. The man had taken her to Alcesa's boarding house, a ramshackle row house on a back street near the docks, and the old woman greeted him with warmth and motherly affection.

"Now, how do you feel? Better, I'd hope." Alcesa sat in a large rocker, sipping from a mug of hot tea.

Tessa nodded and sipped from her own mug: The room was full of earth colors, the lamps illuminating a secure, warmly appointed place. "Yes, thank you very much. You and...Varian."

Alcesa smiled at the mention of the man's name. "Yes, of course, Varian."

"You've known him a long time?"

"Like a son. I first met him when he was still in his teen years. He was a cabin boy, then. Full of cum and vinegar, he was too. He started staying here whenever he put in at Eleusynnia. He's what you might call the son I never had...." Alcesa smiled, sipped her tea.

"Where's he now? Will he be back soon? What's he going to do with me?"

"So many questions! Are you in some kind of trouble, young Tessa? Midnight's no time to be taking a swim in our harbor."

"You answer mine with a question of your own." Tessa paused, pulling her hair away from the side of her face. "He—Varian—he never even asked me *anything*. He just...took care of me."

51

"There aren't many men like Varian," said Alcesa. "He's a special one, all right."

"I'm beginning to think so...." Tessa stared off toward the door where the strange, but gentle, man had exited almost an hour ago. She wondered when he would return and what she would say to him. She wanted to tell this kind old woman what had happened to her, but she feared that it would sound so melodramatic, contrived perhaps. And yet it was true.

She sat, staring at the fire, watching the ever-changing weave of the flames, and she became lost in her memories, in the pain and the indignity which had plagued her for most of her years. There was a part of her which wanted to believe that maybe it could be over now that this Varian Hamer, the legendary knight in white armor, had entered her life. But there was something deeper in her soul, a burning distrust and perhaps even a hatred of all of them. All men. It seemed that there was not one among them who was not driven, motivated, or at least influenced by that thing between his legs.

The door opened and she tensed in her chair, almost afraid to look toward the foyer, where he stood. He paused to hang up his cloak and unbuckle his weapons belt, hanging it over a chair in the hallway. He tried to smile as he entered the room.

"Where've you been?" asked Alcesa. "Our new guest has been worrying over you."

"She should worry about herself. I've been out tracking down the ID's of those bastards that were after you."

"You could have simply asked *me*. I would have told you who they were." Tessa's voice cracked and she felt ashamed.

"And I might not have been able to believe you," said Varian. "This way, I am convinced. By the way, you'll not have to worry about anybody looking for you from *The Silver Girl*...."

"Why not?" Tessa felt tense at the mere mention of the ship's name.

"I've got some friends at the Port Authority. You're listed as killed during a mishap at sea. Along with the fellows that were 'escorting' you in the longboat." Varian smiled and sat down by the fire. "How about some coffee, Alcesa?"

The large woman, smiling, sprang to her feet. "For you, my Varian, anything!" and she laughed as she glided effortlessly into the kitchen.

In a moment she returned with a large glass stein filled with a rich black liquid. The steam eddied and rolled up from its surface as Varian put it to his lips and drank a large mouthful. "It's a cold night. Cooler than I'd thought. You're lucky I was walking down by the docks," he said to Tessa.

"You do that often. Walk alone down there?"

"No, but tonight I was thinking about something. About an odd...'man' I met before sailing out of Mentor. I haven't been able to get the fellow's words out of my head since I met him. Walking down by the water lets me think more clearly."

Tessa did not speak for a few minutes and no one else did either. She watched the man as he sat in the large chair, drinking from the large stein. He was not a huge man, but he gave the impression of being larger than he was because of his whole bearing, his whole way of moving and talking. He was a leader, a thinker, a true anomaly in a world which seemed to have a distinct lack of either of the above. She let her thoughts wander into other areas that were vitally important to her and was thus caught off guard when he spoke to her.

"What's the matter? What're you thinking about?"

"Oh, I was wondering what was going to happen to me now...." She hated herself for saying it. It made her sound so damned helpless, so much the woman-in-distress. Gods, she hated that image!

"Can you fight?"

"Fight?"

"Are you trained in any weapons?" Varian's expression was serious. He was not the kind of man who enjoyed mockery.

"No, I'm afraid not."

"Any sailing experience? Know how to rig a line?"

Tessa laughed. "No, of course not. Eyck is not a country known for its maritime endeavors."

Varian shrugged. "It's not known for much of anything."

"Now you're getting the picture. I'm not trained for much of anything. I was in school for a while, studying to be an interpreter. . . . I have this knack for languages, it seems; but my father. . . he took me out of school to work the farm after my mother died. I studied on my own, but I'm not really good enough to work in the field. At least I don't think I am."

"Languages, eh? That's a fine skill to have, even if everybody does speak G'Rdellian."

"Nesporance and Avestese are almost dialects of G'Rdellian, they're so similar. I'm sure they're all from the same root-language system. The same with Odoän, Scorpinnesk, and Shudris—all the same root language, I'm sure."

Varian nodded. "I pick up a few words here and there, since I'm all over the place. It makes sense to me." He paused for a moment, lighting his pipe. Then: "What about galley help. You can do that, can't you?"

"Cooking? Of course, my father. . ." She let the sentence die. Even the memory of the vile old man made her inwardly shudder. "Why do you ask such a thing?"

"You can't go back where you came from. You have no marketable skills. You need help. Alcesa would be glad to keep you here as long as you like, and maybe you could eventually find work, or perhaps enroll in one of the universities. You are fortunate at least to be in one of the World's finest cities. You know what they say of Eleusynnia: 'Whatever a man might desire, it can be found in *The City of Light.'*"

54

"'From the highest ideal to lowest perversion,'" said Tessa, finishing the quotation.

"Oh, you've heard that one?" Varian smiled. "Well, it's true."

"Yes, I know. I've been thinking of staying in Eleusynnia, but I didn't know Alcesa would put me up. I have no money, you know. I have nothing."

Alcesa shrugged. Varian waved his hand. "I can pay your costs until you get on your feet. Or, you can come with me...."

Tessa tensed in her chair. Varian could not help but notice. "What's wrong?" he asked.

"Nothing. I'm sorry. Nothing." She looked away for a moment. "Why would I come with you?"

"You would come only if you truly wished to. I am bound next for Ques'ryad. It's quite a city and you might want to see it and, later, a little bit more of the world before you decide where you want to be, what you want to do with yourself."

Tessa searched this strange man's eyes before answering. It was clear to her that he spoke sincerely. He was not given to deception and she could sense this. He was genuinely interested in her welfare. And, of course, she did owe him her life, whatever that was worth....

"I don't know," she said slowly. "How could I sail with you?"

"There's never been a crew I've seen that would not welcome the company of a beautiful woman," said Varian, smiling. "And don't take that the wrong way. No harm would come to you.... I'd see to that."

Alcesa laughed. "You can be sure of that, my lady. No one bothers Varian Hamer."

Varian looked embarrassed, but said nothing to refute the old woman's boast.

"I don't know," said Tessa. "I'd have to think about it. How long will you be in Eleusynnia?"

"We sail in two days."

"I'll decide by then. I promise you."

* * *

For the next two days, Varian escorted her about the famed City of Light. There were festivals in various precincts, avenues filled with bazaars and musicians, contests and exhibits. There were museums and galleries, sporting events, and great pieces of architecture to be explored and admired. Varian spoke of the city's great tradition for culture and enlightenment, and she noticed that he spoke with the tongue of an educated man, not the rough, coarsened argot of a common sailor. He was an enigma, this man. She had never known anyone even remotely like him. This she realized as the two days swept by her in a seeming instant. Her memories of the time were a montage of colors and images and sounds. The lyrical music of the orchestra in the Great Park, the pageantry and hue of the Sor Theater, where the morality plays of the First Age were still enacted with as much authenticity as possible, the setting sun playing its dying light about the white-sand shores of the beaches below the city, the gentle lapping surf of the G'Rdellian Sea. Tessa embraced all of these things and she fell in love with the magical city on the sea. It was difficult to imagine leaving such a place if one had a choice, but there was another part of her which saw the man who introduced her to the magic and the wonder. The thought of not seeing him bothered her as such a thought should not have ever bothered her. There was a large world to be seen and to be tasted and touched and smelled. She did not want to do it alone, for she had been alone for such a long, long time.

For Varian, a different set of feelings had rushed into his mind. He too had been alone for a long time, but not in the same sense as Tessa. Varian had chosen a life of solitude of his own free will. It was as though he needed the freedom from responsibility to others so that he could more truly learn about himself. True, he had sailed on every conceivable type of ship, to every known harbor on the Aridard, and true also had he been constantly surrounded by crews of rugged, competent men.

But in truth, too, Varian had been alone in the crowd.

Through all the years, he had never taken the time to get to know any of his mates. The only friend to Varian had been old Furioso, and that relationship seemed to have taken shape more out of inevitability than true desire. Varian and the old man had simply grown accustomed to each other's company.

The women in Varian's life had been nothing more than an endless passage of brief liaisons. Their faces and their bodies were faint blurs in his memory, and only a few of their names could he even remember. It was not that he had used women, not consciously at any rate, but more so that *they* used him. There had never been any mention of *love* (other than the sweaty, urgent, night-desires to "make" it) with any of the women. It was always as though both they and Varian knew that he would be booking passage on another ship quite soon, and that they might never see each other again.

When Varian took the time to think about such relationships, he had always been able to rationalize them thusly: He could not risk the time required to really *know* someone else; it was more important that he first spend his time getting to *know himself*.

But things with Tessa were...different?...yes, definitely. He spent two days with her in Eleusynnia. Two full and complete days. Every hour of every day. And every night. And yet there was not the familiar urgency, the swelling of bodily desire that seemed to cloud all rational thought. There was not the unspoken assent on both parties' part to rush to a dark union and leave their souls somewhere behind.

No. With Tessa, he talked of many things. He asked her questions about herself. He told of his own life and inquired of hers. They shared one another—in mind as well as body—and Varian sensed that it was truly different. Perhaps, he first thought, he was growing "older," as people often told him that he would. Perhaps he was finally feeling comfortable with the person who he had discovered he was? Or, perhaps it was something else entirely: that he sensed he was approaching a turning point in his life, a pivotal, crucial moment when all the things for which he had been unconsciously preparing himself were close at hand....

Varian did not know, but he recalled old Furioso's words about such things. The weapons master believed that everyone was in the World for a purpose, and that some of us came to their purpose early in life, and others late. But we all reached that point in our lives when things come to a sharp, brief, focus, and we know that it is Time. Time to change. To act.

Ever since Varian had spoken with Kartaphilos, he had sensed that things were changing in his life. He knew already that he could no longer be satisfied by simply being a sailor the rest of his days. There was more substance to the world than rolling chops and salty air. He knew that now.

And there was Tessa. Strangely beautiful. Innocent and naïve, and yet worldly-wise. Somehow, she was able to touch him as no woman had ever done before. She was able to reach into him and set off the spark that had been lying dormant for so many years. With a look from her dark eyes, with a brush of her soft fingers on his cheek, with a word. These were the things which made Varian see her for what she might be...for him.

Varian saw these things as they passed the two days in the City of Light, and he dwelled upon them in the dark silence of the nights as she lay sleeping beside him. He made no claims to know what love might be, but something inside him was coming to life, and he suspected what it might be. There was something special about this woman, Tessa of Prend; he was certain of that. It was a specialness that he knew he had only briefly sampled. There were layers of her person that

58

she hinted could be opened to him, and only him. And Varian was interested.

But when he thought more deeply, and honestly, about her, Varian knew that he was more than merely interested. He cared. About her and about what they might share together.

The two days passed swiftly, and Varian did not want it to end there. At the end of the two days, Tessa gave him her decision.

And he was very happy with it.

THREE

It was a simple matter to book Tessa's passage on *The Courtesan*. Both the captain and the first mate smiled when Varian introduced her to them. From that point, it was a "piece of cake," and she assumed her place in the ship's well-appointed galley where she worked with a short, hunchbacked cook by the name of Farle, who produced miracles with the small variety of the ship's stores. A well-fed crew is a happy crew. A simple fact of life.

The voyage westward was an education for Tessa, and she spent many hours on deck with Varian, learning the ways of the merchant mariner. But when he was off-duty, he spent much of his time alone. It was not that he consciously ignored the woman, far from it, actually—he found her very attractive, intelligent, and resourceful among other things—but he had become quite interested in the crate of texts and manuscripts which he had carried on board from Eleusynnia.

Each night, he sat by lamplight in his private cabin and searched for references to *anything* which might tie the loose threads of Kartaphilos' story together. There were so many places of sand, so *few* references to the Riken or Genon; the First Age seemed to be a world awash with legends, fables, and outright falsification. Somewhere along the line, the profession of the historian became distorted into that of a storyteller, and entertainer, to make one forget about the cold night beyond the aura of the campfire.

He debated sharing his search with Tessa, not that he was unable to trust her but that she would not believe him. Certainly she did not understand his need for privacy when he was off watch, and Varian imagined that she was wondering when he would get around to noticing her. *Really* noticing.

But there had been other things to occupy and educate her mind. The passage through the Straits of Nsin was as mysterious and fogbound as ever, and Tessa was entranced by the towering white cliffs on the southern side of the Straits where the great Guns of Kell still loomed as a reminder of the power of the past. The lights of the Voluspa Beacon, just off the coast of the philosopher's city, guided them safely into open waters, where they sailed by their charts and instruments until the coastline of the Isle of Gnarra was cited. Tessa very much wanted to see the port of Cybele and the population of necromancers, which she had heard lived there. Varian was amused. She had spoken of Cybele as if wizards and sorcerers teemed in the streets like rats in a tavern alley.

There had also been a brief encounter with a Behistar raider—a small, but fast, frigate which tested the strength of *The Courtesan*'s cannon. It had been the last engagement for the small black ship.

And now they were putting into port at Ques'ryad. Almost twice the size of any other port on the Aridard, Ques'ryad was a sprawling center of trade, adventure, and cultural exchange. The harbor was filled with ships of every port, flags of every nation cracking in the stiff sea breeze, the docks aswarm with men and exotic cargoes from every corner of the World. Dried meats from the Shudrapur, pelts and furs from trappers north of the Scorpinnian Empire, diamonds from the mines of Kahisma, tapestries and pottery from Asir, musical instruments from Sanda, ironwood from the Kirchou forests, glass sculptures from the Slagland. The riches of the World flowed and swirled like water about the wharves and piers, loaded and unloaded, changed from one ship to the next. Ques'ryad was the nexus, the interchange where all things and all men seemed to eventually converge.

That evening, their first in the port city, Tessa was enthralled with the idea of exploring the town. Varian accompanied her through the winding streets, down the long boulevards, and through the vast parks and gardens. They were surrounded by the spires and obelisks of the city. Temples and museums, monuments and other edifices of great age loomed everywhere. The air was filled with the languages of men of every color and size and belief, almost crackling with the smells of roasted nuts and meats, of flowers, and liquors.

As the midnight hour approached, even Varian felt fatigued, and he begged Tessa the opportunity to visit a tavern for a soft chair and a warming mug of coffee and rum. She smiled and agreed as Varian immediately headed for a favorite roosting place in among the smaller streets, off the beaten pathways of the principal boulevards and commercial routes. On the intersect of two smaller, twisting streets, crowded with shops, was an inn called The White Donzell; it was adorned with a large swinging sign with a painted fresco of one of the beautiful horned creatures beneath the letters.

Inside, there was a large open area where long oak tables had been arranged in orderly rows. The walls were yellowing brick trimmed in brown beams and covered with tapestries and paintings from every country and every age. There was a fine patina of dust and tar from the billowing clouds of burning bac which covered everything, imparting a mellow, lived-in aroma to the place. The floor was covered with sawdust so thick that it was like moss in a shaded forest. There was music— a small ensemble of stringed instruments in a loft above—and, of course, a long bar where three barkeeps were kept eternally busy by hundreds of men and women drinking, laughing, smoking, living.

Varian and Tessa entered, dressed in inconspicuous clothing which tagged them as merchant seamen. No one took more than token interest in their entrance, and they walked uninterrupted to a table next to a large crowd of people who were listening with rapt attention to the tales of a large, loud man dressed in a cloak of silver-gray fur.

"This is a beautiful place!" said Tessa. "I've never seen anything like it."

Varian looked at her. She was bubbling over with wonder and love—love of the magic in the world. She was like a child, and he was beginning to like her very much for it.

They spoke of their day in Ques'ryad, occasionally having to half-yell their words over the music, the explosive laughter and banter of the crowd at the next table. It was not long before Varian found himself paying more attention to the rough, slightly high-pitched voice of the old man in the fur than to Tessa and her continuous exclamations about the city.

Rather than be rude, Varian tried to draw her into his sphere of interest. "Look at that fellow," he said, pointing to the man.

"He is quite a character, isn't he?" said Tessa, laughing.

The man sat at the far end of the table, wearing his fur cape like a royal cloak. He was surrounded by a semicircle of ardent listeners and it did seem that he was holding a kind of narrator's court with them. His face was tough and baked by the sun like the wrinkled surface of an almond. His hair the same silver-gray color as his animal-pelt cloak, and his eyes were a fiery blue that seemed to belong to a man much younger than his obvious years. He had a large hawkish nose, bent and beaked and probably broken more than once, above a large full mouth which was unobscured by a carefully trimmed salt-and-pepper beard. He was loud, but he spoke with careful emphasis on just the right words so that he kept the attention of his audience always on the edge. He had the knack of the storyteller and he reveled in it.

By the man's side was a much smaller and younger man, who listened with rapt attention to everything the old fellow said. Occasionally, the old man would nudge him or ask him to recall with pleasure a certain facet of a story, and the short man would nod and wink and laugh with the intimacy of a true sidekick. Varian studied him for a moment, wondering if he looked familiar, trying to place the face with a name or a location. He was short, but very stocky, musculature in evidence beneath the thick clothing. His eyes and his hair were jet black and his skin shone with oily perspiration. He had an engaging smile, very white teeth, sharp, angular nose and jaw. He was handsome, but in an unfinished, crude kind of way.

Varian noticed, however, that the small sidekick, while very animated, did not speak. This was either out of deference and respect to his master and chief storyteller, or else the man was mute.

"...and the mutations are *still* goin' on in the Baadghizi Vale. Three winters back, Raim and I were there—weren't we, my small fellow?—and we saw cockroaches the size of your boot, walkin' around like they owned the place. And they do! But it's not the roaches that'll get you, no sir. It's the lizards, by the gods, it's the friggin' lizards!"

Someone took the bait, asked about the lizards, and the man was off again.

"Big, ugly, scaly things! They're slinkin' and screwin' in the Vale to beat all! Pretty soon they'll be so many of them, they'll be crawlin' over each other's back, spend their whole lives never touchin' the ground. And I mean they're big, too. Some of them are learnin' to stand up on their hind legs like a man. Get to be five or six ems high, and they can outrun you and have you for breakfast before you can say Ben Hurlendsesk!"

"How'd you get away?" someone asked with a smile.

"Me? I'll get away from *every*thing, 'cept Mr. Bones!"

The man in the silver fur threw back his head and laughed. "No, you see, them lizards are big and fast and hungry, for sure, but they're godsawful dumb, too! You can fool 'em with tricks that even a hangclaw wouldn't fall for. In fact, I caught a big one in a trap I'd set, brought back the head to a king north of the Scorpinnian. Called himself Richer the Third, he did. Funny-lookin' little fellow with a withered arm, but mean as a cat! Gave 'im that big bugger's head and took off from there. That's when Raim and I, we teamed up with an expedition on the Sunless Sea. Ship was *The Pea-Pod,* ever heard of her? No, I'd feature you haven't, but she was a fine-rigged thing. Captained by a crazy man the name of Ajax. Raim got into a fight with one of the gunner's on board—a big illustrated man, forget his name, and they cut some new pictures into each other's flesh, didn't you, my lad?"

The man laughed again and gestured for the small, dark Raim to display the knife wounds on the left side of his chest. After an appreciative round of ooohs and aaahs, the old man continued his tale. It was a nonstop, rollicking sea story, and Varian was caught up in it, despite himself.

Varian had heard variations of these stories for years. You did not sail the World, frequent the watering holes of every fellow nomad, and *not* hear them, but there was something different about this man's delivery, his style. And most important, his appearance. He *looked* as if he had done the things he said. Varian's keen eye for detail did not miss the thick, calloused palms, the "character" lines in the face, the young, vigilant eyes, and the heavy musculature of the shoulders and the neck. This old man was a man of action and experience; his knack for the well-turned tale was only a colorful talent, an added attraction.

"What's wrong?" asked Tessa, reaching out and touching Varian's sleeve.

"Oh, nothing. I was just watching him, listening..."

Tessa laughed and sipped from her stein. "You don't believe him, do you?"

"No, not everything. I never believe all that *any* man says."

"But some things, yes?"

"Of course." Varian gestured at the old man. "Just look at him. I mean *really* look at him. He's real. He's been there—wherever it is. He's like Ques'ryad itself: there's the smell and the look of adventure about him, and danger, too."

"Varian, I think you *do* believe him!" She smiled, gave him a mock reproachful look.

"He is an interesting fellow, you can't deny that," said Varian, looking once again to the table where the narration continued.

"...some say they were *golems,* but they're probably not livin' things at all," said the old man, his eyes gliding suspensefully back and forth in his sockets. "For my money, they were *robots!*"

Someone in the crowd laughed, followed quickly by the guffaws and doubting remarks of others. Varian felt himself tense at the mention of the word.

"So don't believe me! What hang do I give? I know it *could* be a robot, 'specially since I seen one myself!"

More laughter and general loud commentary. The crowd believed that the old man was now openly playing with them, slipping from the mode of tall-tale teller to that of jester, buffoon.

Everyone laughed but Varian. In an instant he was swept back to the moment on board *The Courtesan* when the...the thing pulled back its robes and revealed its amber-glass chest, the sparkling patterns of the printed circuitry and LEDs.

"No, it's true, I tell you!" said the man. "You can ask Raim, here. He saw him, too!"

Raim nodded his head solemnly.

"I was comin' back from the wilderness north of the Shudrapur. Raim and me, we were lookin' for First Age pieces for this merchant in Borat. Didn't find a thing so far, when we stop at this outpost near the borders—about five hundred kays from Babir—and we get to talkin' with some of the villagers. You learn to listen to what them village people have to say. They might not say things as nicely as we do, but they make a lot of sense, and they ain't got nobody to impress. What I mean is, they don't lie...got no reason to."

The silver-furred man paused to drink from his large stein, and Varian could feel the apprehension and the anxiety in the air. He could feel the expectations of all who listened to the tale. Tessa reached out, touching Varian's wrist, and he flinched.

"So, anyhow, we get into the outpost, and one of the trappers, he tells me there's been a monk, or somebody like that, passin' through and askin' for *me!* Now, I got to think this is pretty odd, 'cause there ain't hardly no one knows I'm out there, or what I'm doin'. And surely there's no monks that know me. I'm not what you'd call a religious man." He paused and looked skyward, then made a halting sign of the star on his breast. Everyone laughed and he waited for it to subside before continuing.

"A few days go by, and Raim and myself, we're just restin' up, gettin' some good cooked food and like that. I snoop around a bit and find that the fellow's been lookin' for me—his name's Cartor Fillus, and he's supposed to be a messenger from my employer, Marduk, the Salasan of Borat. Now I *am* confused! We're thousands of kays from Zend Avesta, near impossible to track down, and Marduk's supposed to be sendin' me a message. It was crazy, see? So I decide to wait it out in the village to see if this fellow shows up, 'cause now I sure as shit want to talk to 'im."

Varian was now only half listening to the narrative. He *knew* now that the old man was not lying. There was no coincidence so close. Kartaphilos. Cartor Fillus. No, it was the same man, the same *thing*. What did it all mean? For the first time in his life, Varian felt as though he were losing control of things, as if he might be being manipulated by forces greater than he could understand.

"...and it's night, see? Raim is sleepin' and I got the watch. There's nothin' but dark and cold all around our tent, and sure enough I hear somethin' out there. I have a 9-mil sidearm that'll put a hole in a man the size of a pie pan, right? So I pull it out and aim out there. I always fire first and talk about it later. And I'm about to squeeze off a few rounds in the direction of the noise when I hear my name bein' called...real formal, like I was in the House of Salasans: 'Stoor of Hadaan, I greet you. I come in peace.' So I tell him to come out into the light, and out steps this old man in a robe, a hood up over his head, sure as shit lookin' like a monk. 'Cartor Fillus?' I asks, and he nods his head. So I bring him into the camp and offer him some drink, but he didn't take none. We make small talk awhile, then I asked him how he found me way out there, and he won't say exactly, says he has 'his special ways.' I figured that meant he wasn't about to give away any trade secrets, so I let it go. Then he tells me that he don't really work for Marduk. I also figured that, but I wasn't about to tell him...."

The old man paused to drink again, and Varian studied the faces of his audience. There was everything there—disbelief, amusement, rapt attention, drunken ignorance. Yet they all listened.

"...but then a funny thing happens, and I *know* this is going to sound like I rigged it up in my dreams, but listen up: I hear a sound out in the darkness, some big branches breakin' quick, like there's somethin' out there, moving real fast-like. But before I can raise up my 9-mil piece, there's this big shape flying out of the black woods.

"Old Cartor, he stands up and catches the thing right in the chest. It was a cragar, the biggest, meanest one I ever saw, almost three ems long! Hit old Cartor with its claws out and fangs ready to chomp. I expected the old man to be torn pretty much in half before he hit the ground, but it wasn't like that.

"The cragar's on top of him, ripping and slashing like they do, right? I got time, only a second or two, but that's all I need to squeeze off two rounds. Wango! The cragar's head's gone! Pieces flyin' all over the place.

"But that ain't the end of it. I walk over and kick the carcass off poor old Cartor Fillus, expecting to see a meat market, right? And he sits up, trying to gather up the folds of his robes. 'Thank you,' he says to me.

"By this time I would have normally fell out, 'cause there's no man alive that could have taken that kind of hit from a night-stalkin' cragar....But, you see, I already knew that this Cartor Fillus was *no man at all!*

"That critter had torn up his clothes bad, and while he tried to gather them up, I saw what was underneath. Metal! And glass! So thick and clear, like it was topaz! And underneath, it was ablaze with light and power!

"I step back as he tries to pull his clothes up about him, but he knows and I knows and by now even Raim knows—'cause he heard the cragar coming out of the woods. So we all stand there lookin' at each other for a minute or two, then the robot says: 'I would have told you eventually that I was not human, but I suppose this demonstrates that a bit more dramatically.' And I told him it sure did, and what, by the way, did a robot want with me, trackin' me down in the wilderness, especially when there weren't supposed to be any robots around anyway?

"Well, he sat back and he told me a story, which he made me promise not to repeat to anyone—and naturally, I promised, since I am a man of my word, and—"

The crowd had burst into laughter, thinking that old Stoor had reached a punch line of sorts. He could not, of course, tell the robot's story because there *was* no robot. A tall tale, then, to be enjoyed by all.

"Wait a minute! You got this one wrong! This ain't no story...."

But everyone continued to laugh and wink at each other, nodding their heads knowingly. Several of the number drifted off to refill their steins, others turned to each other for smaller, more private conversations. As if by some unspoken signal, Stoor's turn in the spotlight had come abruptly to an end. The old man stared at his short, dark-haired companion. They shrugged at one another, stood up, and headed toward the bar.

As they passed the table of Varian and Tessa, the merchant marine touched the old man's sleeve.

Stoor looked down at him quizzically.

"I believe you, old man," said Varian.

"You want an award, maybe?" Stoor turned to go but was stopped by the hard, fast grip of the young sailor.

"Please," said Varian. "I am serious. I *know* you tell the truth...about the...the robot."

Stoor smiled and looked at Raim. "And how might you know that?"

"The Guardian," said Varian. "He came to me, and he told me about the Guardian."

The expression rapidly changed on Stoor's face from amusement to shock, then quickly to acceptance. Sitting down on the bench next to Varian, Stoor looked quickly from Varian to the young woman, then back.

"It's all right if she knows," said Varian.

"Knows what?" said Tessa, grabbing his wrist.

"You tell me what you know," said Stoor, his eyes boring into Varian with the intensity of a trapped animal.

"I shall tell you everything," said Varian.

And he did.

FOUR

Needless to say, after listening to Varian's tale, Stoor and Raim were convinced of several things: that Cartor Fillus and Kartaphilos were one and the same, that the robot's story was consistent down to the smallest detail, and that it might be a good idea to set out in search of the mysterious Citadel.

There were, however, some "terms" which would have to be worked out.

Stoor's primary objection was the presence of Tessa in the group, not because she was a woman—Stoor had always been a great admirer of women—but rather her lack of any skills that might assist their expedition. Her facility for language was her saving grace, and Varian repeatedly used this in her defense. It *was* a valuable asset to have someone who could communicate with practically anyone they might encounter.

There was another reason, however, why Varian wanted to include Tessa on the expedition. He was falling in love with her. Varian Hamer—no stranger to women—was able to admit to himself that it was happening. He thought that perhaps the present situation forced the issue, but it did not matter. The idea of not being with Tessa, or leaving her behind in some strange and hostile city, was unthinkable. Therefore, it must be love. So be it.

If old Stoor suspected any such motive, he kept silent

about it. Either he respected the sentiment, or he was afraid of offending a man such as Varian. No matter.

The other thing to be decided was the object of the entire mission. Stoor and Raim had been soldiers of fortune for many seasons, and they had difficulty in thinking in terms of anything but money and its attendant mercenary aspects. In the past, all their expeditions were financed by an outside party; their part in the plan, a given, a guarantee. But in this new plan, there was a total risk. To bring in yet another member to the expedition would divide the spoils, plus risk competition (or worse) from unknown parties.

All these things were discussed at length in the bars of Ques'ryad, in its courtyards and plazas, and its sumptuous inns and liveries.

It was decided that passage by ship would be a very bad idea. A sailing vessel is a microcosm in which secrets are hard to keep, especially when they are held by more than one person. As convenient and safe and quick as a ship might be, it was ruled out. The first mate of *The Courtesan* was thus notified that Varian and the galley helper, Tessa, would not be making the trip back to Mentor.

The prospect of covering the known World on foot, or even on horseback, was a dizzying one, however; and Stoor set about solving this problem by contacting a wealthy Zend Avestan merchant, who owed several "favors" to Stoor of Hadaan. It seems as if, in past years, Stoor had been employed to find First Age artifacts for the merchant's collection and private museum, located on his villa overlooking the Grünewald Bight. There were many times when Stoor had been requested to bring back very specific items, and when he succeeded, the merchant offered to reward him with special bonuses; Stoor had always declined, knowing that someday he would be able to "collect" on the owed favors.

The time to collect had come.

Ten years previous, Stoor had uncovered a First Age machine under the shifting sands that lapped upon the

74

barricades of the Maaradin Fortress. It was a personnel carrier: semiarmored, fully treaded, light armament, and completely functional. It had somehow escaped destruction long enough to be interred by the ever-changing landscape, thereby preserved in the ultradry climate. The carrier had been a momentous discovery and regarded as a marvel of the First Age. It was in excellent condition, although the moving and electronic parts of the engine and ancillary equipment were corroded, even deteriorated to some extent. In other words, it would not run.

But if it would ever run again, it would run in Zend Avesta. It was in that country where the mind was given the most freedom, and it was a place where *change* was not deterred by hidebound tradition. Zend Avestan scientists and inventors, upon invitation by the wealthy merchant, crawled all over the ancient machine. They learned greatly from its construction, from its basic principles of self-propulsion, and it was from this discovery that the tractors and simple vehicles now seen in Zend Avesta can be traced. The country's inventors soon developed an engine that would function on the methane derived from feces, thus replacing the petrochem engine originally found in the carrier.

The time came when the carrier was only a curiosity, a prototype, from which far more practical machines were produced. And so it spent most of its days on the first floor of the merchant's private museum, where attendants daily polished it.

Until, that is, the day Stoor of Hadaan paid the merchant an unexpected call.

That afternoon, Stoor and Varian sat in the front cab of the vehicle as it trundled across the open countryside east of the Bight. Tessa and Raim were busy in the rear compartment storing gear and supplies.

"I still can't believe *anyone* could owe you such a favor," said Varian.

Stoor threw back his head and laughed.

"No, really. I mean, this is incredible!" Varian looked over the vehicle like a little boy with a new plaything. It was a mechanical wonder! A marvel to which he doubted he would ever grow accustomed.

"Not really," said Stoor. "Not when you figure my friend had no real use for it anymore. His folks can reproduce this one whenever he wishes it. What the world needs now is tractors, not personnel carriers! Besides, I promised him I'd bring him back somethin' far more valuable than this damn machine!"

"Gods! What was that?"

Stoor laughed again. "Does it matter? If we find what we're lookin' for, that merchant will be the least of our worries."

"Where do we go first?"

"Logically, we look for all the great deserts and similar barren territories. We both got the same clues—it's in a sandy place, right?"

"Suppose it's not anywhere in the known World?"

"You mean somewhere beyond...?"

Varian nodded.

"Then we go there too," said Stoor. "I've been out pretty far in the Manteg. Seems to go on forever, though. Don't know *any* man that's ever been across the whole thing. Same for the Slagland."

"But we might have to do it. Right?"

"It's possible. Anything's possible. Get me that map."

Stoor pointed to a small steel box on the floor of the cab. Varian opened it and pulled out a map of the World inked on a folded piece of oilskin. Its folds were deep creases and the edges were worn with use. It was a silent testament to the lifetime of Stoor's travels.

"Now, I figure we work south a bit and cut into the Samarkesh Burn. Hell of a place that is!"

"You been there?"

"Only when I had to. Raiders chased me through there years ago. Before the Interdict on them animals. Before I met Raim. It was tough, but I made it." Stoor threw in the throttle and gunned the methane engine, which whined as it revved up to traverse a steep rise they had just reached.

Varian let the conversation pause for a moment. If he pressed the old man too much, he would be launched into another highly detailed story, and he wasn't in the mood for it. Varian was interested in the adventure at hand, in the types of equipment they had, in the techniques necessary for desert survival.

"Tell me about the Finder," he said finally, pointing to a set of controls on the dash console.

"Ain't much to tell. I don't know much about how it works. Just that it does, that's all."

"There were sailors in Elahim who were experimenting with radio things something like this. They said they would be able to detect ships beyond the horizon, out of visual range. Is it like that?"

"Better than that. Them First Agers were a slick bunch, I keep telling you. This thing here lights up whenever we come within range of any large metal or stone object, and this panel here will print out information which will tell us the location."

"What's the range of the thing?"

"Pretty far. About four hundred kays."

Varian shood his head. The technology which produced such a thing bordered upon magic. In fact, as far as he was concerned it might as well *be* magic. "Is it always turned on?"

Stoor nodded. "It'll start beepin' if anything comes into range. Then we got the choice of either trackin' it down and checkin' it out, or passin' it by. With my map and knowledge of the areas, we can bypass lots of crap, 'cause I'll know what's supposed to be there."

He pointed to the map. "Like right there. There's a bombed-out monastery right around there. If we keep on this course, it'll show up on the Finder."

"And we'll go past without having to check it, right?" Varian studied the screen, which glowed with a bright yellow-green light.

"Yep."

"But wait a minute..." said Varian. "Suppose the Guardian is located somewhere in the ruins. *Beneath* the monastery, perhaps? And we went by...?"

"Then we wouldn't find it, would we?" Stoor laughed.

Varian said nothing. He didn't understand.

"Listen, boy," said the old man. "That monastery's been there a long time and *everybody* knows it's there. I've crawled over every stone in the place and so have a lot of schoolboys by this time. If the Guardian's there, well, he's hidden so well that nobody's going to find him!"

"I see..." said Varian, reaching for his pouch and pipe.

"The way I figure it," said Stoor. "This Citadel...this place where the Guardian lays out...is in some god-awful place where no men ever go. Else it would've been turned up by this time. See what I mean? It *wants* to be found, or it wouldn't send that robot around to keep tellin' its story. See what I mean?" Stoor looked over at Varian for a moment then continued to wrestle with the controls, navigating along the edge of a wide arroyo.

"Then we're going to be traveling through some territory that you've never seen before. Possibly that *no* man has ever seen before...."

"You have a funny way of makin' the obvious sound kind of profound," said Stoor, laughing at his own wit.

It *was* funny, the way he said it, and Varian couldn't help but smile himself.

"How far are we from the Burn?"

"About three hours before we hit the first part of it. I figure to swing south and avoid most of the Behistar Republic. There's no sense in tanglin' horns with any of that wild bunch there. We'll check out the Burn, then if we come up short, head east to the Hesen River. From there, it's only a little bit to the Ironfields."

"You been there many times?"

"Ironfields? Yeah, sure. But I ain't seen it all. Ain't

no man alive that's seen it all. It goes on and on. It's the biggest single thing I've ever seen in the World except for maybe the Slaglands. Don't know which is bigger 'cause they both seem to just go on forever."

"I've never seen it. It must be awesome."

"Awesome? Maybe that's the word, I don't know. You see all them wrecks, all the bones...you think: What the hell ever happened here? Who could've been so powerful?" Stoor shook his head. "It makes you think that whoever they were—the men of the First Age—they were a far better bunch than us. Than we'll ever be. Yeah, I've never been to the Ironfields without havin' a scary feelin' come over me...."

The Finder alarm on the control panel beeped into life. The screen indicated a larger mass south of their current position.

"That's the monastery. See, what'd I tell you? If you didn't have me along, you might go down there and waste a lot of supplies and time." The old man laughed again.

Varian looked at him closely, trying to figure him out. It might be difficult to spend an indefinite amount of time with him. His manner was abrupt and, although straightforward, hard to take in large doses. He was authoritative and was obviously used to being in charge of things. Varian usually did not get along well with men such as that, yet Stoor's age and inestimable experience seemed to temper the personality differences.

But Varian wondered what motivated him. He seemed to have the wanderlust, the *need* to be moving and constantly discovering. Stoor would be seemingly just as happy off in the Manteg hunting sphinders or lizards. And yet though he wanted to find the Citadel, he did not seem to exhibit any of the urgency or excitement that such a quest should instill.

They sat in silence for a while as Varian continued to think about the group he had aligned himself with. Stoor was something of a mystery and would continue to be until time unwound his true nature. Raim, his inseparable companion, was quite a bit simpler to understand.

From what Varian had been able to pick up in bits of offhand reference to the small, muscular man, Raim had been a Maaradin courier for a company in Borat. His reliability and courage were renowned and he often drew the toughest assignments, transporting diplomatic pouches throughout the World. That is, until the time when his small frigate was overtaken by a Behistar Raider and he was taken prisoner rather than killed outright because one of the officers recognized him as an upper-echelon courier. Since he had dispatched his packet over the side at the first sign of the Raiders, there was no concrete information or evidence Raim could have given them. But they still took him back to their renegade headquarters and tortured him.

Raim, although he would have been faithful to the last and would not have divulged any information, knew nothing of value to the Raiders that they did not already know. As punishment for not cooperating, they cut out his tongue and banished him to a cruel death in the Samarkesh Burn. It was there that old Stoor had found him, the old man himself on the run from the barbaric Raiders. Stoor nursed him back to health and carried him out of the Burn, where they met a platoon of the Home Militia out of the Maaradin Fortress. Raim swore his life to Stoor and had served him unswervingly ever since. That had been almost twenty years ago, and it had proved to be a perfect marriage. That last thought made Varian wonder about the two men's sexual preferences, and he let the possibilities dwindle out of mind without really caring what the true situation was.

Tessa also filled his thoughts. They were now locked into a journey which would keep them in close company twenty-four hours a day. It was going to be a test for them, for everyone. They would be traveling harsh, unknown territory, and there would be no place to go to be alone for any large amounts of time. Everyone would get to know everyone else intimately, and there would be the usual discoveries—the good ones and the bad ones about who did what, and how, to each other's pleasure or distress. She was a special person to him. Varian found himself thinking of her at the oddest moments and he knew what that meant. His life had been a series of hellos and good-byes, and in the final analysis he had always known that he had lived for himself, that he had fought and killed and rambled along for his own survival only. He had never taken the time to think about anyone else, and yet he was doing it now.

Looking over at Stoor, who squinted against the glare, armwrestling the controls of the vehicle and bouncing in the padded seat, Varian snapped out of his thoughts. "I'm going in the back for a while. See if I can help out," he said. Stoor nodded an okay; and Varian, easing out of his seat, headed for the rear compartment. When he got there, he told Raim to take his place in the front cab; the little man grinned and departed.

"What is it?" asked Tessa, who looked up from her work. "Did we find something already?" She smiled at her little joke.

Varian sat down beside and put his arm around her. "No, nothing yet. I just wanted to be with you, that's all."

She put her head on his shoulder and he smelled the natural perfumes of her hair, felt her tensing against him, against her will. He knew some of the things about her life, which had wounded her so terribly, and he prayed that he would not fail her.

The vehicle bounced and rolled from side to side as it conquered the rugged hillsides. Varian held on to her, saying nothing, knowing that it was not necessary. At that moment, both of them knew, there was only one thing that was really important—that they were together.

FIVE

The Citadel did not lie within the Samarkesh Burn.

Stoor spent three methodical weeks crisscrossing the expansive, deadly sand. Thousands of square ems and nothing but the killing heat. The time spent had not been unbearable as one might expect, however. If anything, the group seemed to grow more comfortable with one another.

Varian thought that the utter hostility of the environment may have been an unsensed influence which forced the team to gravitate toward one another. Faced with the bleak, unrelenting cruelty of the Burn, everyone seemed to be seeking out the security that companionship and good cheer can bring.

The evenings were filled with storytelling sessions around an open fire which held the searing chill of the desert night at bay. Stoor was a wellspring of adventures, fables, and morality tales. If one could believe even half of his stories, one would have to believe in a far more interesting world than what actually existed.

"Adventure is where you find it" was one of Stoor's favorite expressions.

Trite, to be sure. But also quite true if your name was Stoor of Hadaan.

While they were moving eastward, finally leaving the Samarkesh Burn, adventure found *them*. Sweeping down on horseback from a small range of dunes came a band of Behistarian Raiders. There were perhaps twenty in number and they advanced upon the personnel carrier with no more fear than had it been a sedan chair laden with an old woman. If one must give any credit at all to the Raiders, it must be said then that they are truly fearless.

Although some would call them simply stupid barbarians, we shall give them the benefit of the doubt.

Varian was at the controls at the time and he was motoring along at a crisp eighty kays, creating a welcome breeze within the cab. Tessa was in the passenger seat, dozing, while Stoor and Raim remained in the rear section, sleeping. When Varian saw the Raiders, he called out for Stoor and Raim, who entered the front cab immediately.

Tessa was given control of the vehicle, and the three men prepared their First Age weapons: Varian's pistol, Stoor's semi-automatic rifle, and Raim's clip-loading scope rifle. Although Varian was dreadfully short on ammunition, the old man and his sidekick had spent a lifetime collecting rounds for their weapons and literally carried more ammunition than food on the journey. Stoor had said: "The food won't do us any good if we don't have the bullets to keep us alive to eat it."

How true....

The personnel carrier must have seemed like an easy target to the slope-browed thugs on horseback. It was long and shaped like a trapezoid, its wide treads chewing up the sand, kicking out rooster tails in its wake. There were no obvious armaments, no turrents or barrels, bristling from its sides. It must have looked like a piece of cake.

But it was not.

As soon as the horsemen drew within range of Raim's scope rifle, he started picking them off. Despite the random pitching of the carrier and the motion of the horsemen, Raim proved to be an excellent marksman, bringing down five riders before they were within range of Stoor's semi. By that time, however, they had correctly assessed the carrier's firepower and had fanned out so that they would make more difficult targets. Varian was the last to be able to fire because of the limited accuracy of his sidearm at long distances. By the time he could shoot, you could almost count the nose hairs of the enemy, and there were still seven of them left.

There was a clatter on the roof of the vehicle as one of the riders boarded. Stoor indicated as much and Varian headed for the hatch which opened on top, unsheathing his shortsword in the same motion. The man on top was no match for a student of Furioso, *the* weapons master of the modern world. Within seconds the bandit's head had been separated from its shoulders and rolled into the vehicle's wake. On top, Varain noted the Raiders, too, possessed several weapons but they appeared to be primitive hammerlocks. Probably copies of museum pieces, and therefore unreliable and just as dangerous to the shootist as the intended victim.

The carrier had a blind side—the rear—and it was from that direction that the remaining six Raiders now rode in single file. Their obvious plan was to overtake the vehicle and board en masse hopefully overwhelming Varian. Stoor had by this time joined Varian on the roof and was ripping the air with his semi weapon. The problem with the gun was its small-caliber rounds which seemed to be having trouble penetrating the body armor of the bandits. He inflicted arm wounds on the two lead riders, but that was all. And considering that the Behistars were *very* tough, and *very* big fellows, that kind of wounding was not going to stop them.

Stoor advised that they let the Raiders board so that they could be properly dispatched of. Varian was not of the same opinion, feeling that as long as there was some distance between them and the large pursuers, they had a better chance of survival. But Raim then joined them on the roof, and there was a quick vote taken.

Varian lost, and the Raiders were allowed to close the gap. It was then that Varian was treated to a fighting display that was truly as spectacular as anything old Furioso could have ever been capable of. Little Raim became a blur of sweating flesh and flashing steel. The first two Raiders had barely grappled on to the edge of the carrier when Varian and Raim descended upon them. Varian saw a heavily muscled arm separated from the armored body of the first attacker, quickly followed by his head. Raim's sword was as sharp as a Vaisyan palace guard's.

It took a bit longer for Varian to parry and riposte his attacker's initial assaults, then he caught him with a side-slashing stroke through the waist and kidneys. Sloppy, but effective. The man went down.

The remaining four Raiders decided to call it a day and started to fall away from the carrier, but Raim picked them all off with his scoped weapon. Varian was disposed to let them escape, but Stoor feared they would bring back a large enough force to eventually overwhelm the trio.

It was, as adventures go, not a great one, but it was extremely instructive. It proved that each man could now respect the other and place more than a small amount of trust in that man's protecting the other's life. It also showed that the three men worked well together as a team, despite the differences in culture, personality, and age.

Varian was beginning to think that they might, after all, be successful.

This feeling persisted and was reinforced when they traveled through the remainder of the Behistar Republic without further incident. Either the absence of the first band of Raiders had stirred up enough respect for the carrier and its crew that the rest of the bandits kept their distance, or they were simply fortunate enough to have avoided anymore dangerous characters.

They had been traveling for more than a full moon cycle when Varian picked up the first traces of the Ironfields on the Finder Screen.

"The Finder's going mad," he said loudly to anyone who could hear.

Stoor ambled forward into the cabin. "Ironfields, dead ahead. Ever see it?"

Varian shook his head. "No. Heard plenty of stories, though."

"Ain't the same. I remember the first time I was through there....Ever hear of Giulio Seezar or....uh, General Patent?"

"No, who are they?"

"Couple of military men I used to travel with when I was a lot younger. Between the two of them, they knew just about all there was to know about fightin'...."

Varian continued to watch the terrain ahead, but spoke easily. "Well, what about them?"

"Oh, yeah! Well I was with them when we came on to the Ironfields. Sun was just goin' down, and we were droppin' down out of G'Rdellia. There's no tellin' how far it stretches; it just goes on and on."

"I've been thinking about it a lot," said Varian. "Do you think it's possible that the great battle that was fought there...do you think it might have been the Riken?"

"And the Genonese?" said Stoor. "Sure, I thought about it. Makes a lot of sense to me. There's so many stories about the 'fields' that nobody knows for sure what really went on there. Some even say that there've been hundreds, maybe even *thousands,* of battles fought there...like it's some kind of magnetic place that *draws* men to it when they sense the time for a 'final confrontation.'"

"Like birds in migration..." said Varian.

"Or lemmings, runnin' to cliffs to kill themselves," said Stoor. "You ever hear them stories. Crazy. Just plain *crazy* little critters!"

Varian was not positive he knew what the old man

87

was talking about, having never heard of "lemmings," but he nodded as if he had. Varian was not in the mood for another story right then, especially about crazy little animals.

The old man looked at the screen where the indicators were illuminating the first markers of the Ironfields, then he checked the sun's position in the sky.

"If we can keep up this pace, we'll probably hit the 'fields by sundown. That seems kind of appropriate, don't it? Kind of poetic-like, I'd say."

Experienced traveler that he was, old Stoor was almost precisely correct in estimating the time of visual contact with the Ironfields. Raim was at the controls and Tessa was in the passenger seat when it happened.

She called out to the others, who entered the cab to see the first dark, crumpled silhouettes on the horizon. The vehicle rambled closer as a light breeze carried warm air through the cab. Sand eddied and capped like sea foam around the twisted hulks, which rose up from the sand like grave markers. The sun was setting and the temperature was dropping rapidly—as though heralding their entrance to a place which lay beyond the limits of space and time.

Images and impressions crowded into Varian's mind; he watched the looming shapes grow larger under the vehicle's approach. Words and emotions fought for place and sense, but he had the feeling of being overwhelmed. They were entering a place of mystery and of myth...

...a place of death.

Nothing moved. Nothing lived in the Ironfields. As the machine moved deeper into the vast hulk yard, a silence descended upon them. Even Stoor was quiet as the group privately took in the horrible tableau. It was an unending gallery, filled with mazelike corridors of the grotesque, the unspeakable. A montage still life of end-moments for men and their machines.

A burned-out tank with a carbonized skeleton still

frozen in that slice of time when it had been a man struggling to be free of the glowing-hot hatch.

The twisted, rusting remains of a great-engined aircraft lying in the vanguard of a plowed-up V of land, marking its last touchdown.

A circular pool of superheated sand, now glazed over to form a diamond-hard slab, its smoothness interrupted by the eruption of a large, twisted piece of steel. The image is of a piece of untitled and very *avant-garde* sculpture.

Machines and pieces of machines litter the sand like dead leaves. The wind slips easily through the countless edges and angles, occasionally rising to produce an eerie music which is a combination of a wail and the phrases of an atonal sonata.

If one believed in them, the place could be aswarm with ghosts. The eidolons of a million soldiers crowd the open spaces, all drifting in the stoop-shouldered half step of forgotten tramps; as though condemned to shamble aimlessly through the ruins forever.

Varian was the one to break the cold silence.

"It's like this all over? I can't believe it...."

"Oh yeah, you'd better believe it," said Stoor. "It goes on like this! On and on and on...thousands, probably *hundreds* of thousands of square kays."

"It's like a museum," said Tessa. "So cold and sterile. It's like we don't belong here. Don't you get that feeling?"

"I've had that feeling," said Varian, looking at the incredible vista of destruction. As a trained fighter, he could understand the necessity for arms; he could respect the power of the machines and armies which had gathered here; he could even feel a twinge of the excitement, the *glory* which must have hung in the air like a burning mist. But all that notwithstanding, even Varian was horrified at the bleak testament of the Ironfields.

It was the ultimate metaphor. The final image. The

lasting momument to man's need to study war once more.

"Look at the Finder," said Tessa, pointing to the screen where a flurry of blips danced like snowflakes. "It's going crazy!"

Stoor reached out, turning down the gain. "We'll have to fine-tune it, adjust it so it will only be sensitive to electromagnetics."

"Can you do that?" Varian looked at the old man, wondering if this was the preamble to another tale.

Stoor nodded. *"Raim* can. You don't spend twenty years in Zend Avesta, hanging around the World's most inventive folk, without learning *something.*"

"What exactly are you talking about?" Tessa looked at him while Raim continued to navigate among the ruins.

"All the old First Age stuff was run on little pieces of wire and chipboard. They called 'em 'crickets' 'cause that's what they looked like. These little things sent out specific signals and the Finder can pick them up, if there's any around. It just has to be told what to look for, see?"

"Right," said Varian. "We don't need it to locate objects ahead anymore. We can *see* them plain enough. But if one of these wrecks is really the Citadel or the Guardian, we'd never know it."

"We could spend a lifetime checking out each wreck," said Tessa.

"All our lifetimes," said Stoor, looking out the windshield. He rubbed his beard, eyed the sky for a moment, then spoke again. "Listen, why don't we pack it in for the night? Raim can adjust the Finder. We'll make camp. A good meal and plenty of rest. We'll be busy for quite a while in here."

Everyone agreed and the vehicle slowly came to a stop under the shadow of a great machine which had moved on large spiked wheels, now transformed into pinwheels of iron oxide.

* * *

The sky was high and cloudless as he walked with her on the perimeter of the camp. The stars were bright and cold above them, and the lyrical notes of Raim's flutelike *arthis* wove expertly among the sheets of night silence. She held his hand tightly, and he could sense her on the brink of trembling.

"Cold?"

"No, it's not that."

"Tessa, do you fear me?" His voice was calm and matter of fact. "Is that it, then? Or is it this place—this thing that we are doing?"

"Maybe all of those things....I don't know, Varian. I've been thinking, and things are not right. I thought that my life was going to be different after I met you. After you saved me..."

"And it *isn't...?*" Sometimes Varian had the feeling that all women were of a similar essential nature that would be forever a mystery to men.

"No, wait. Listen to me. *You* know my life. I've never had any control over it. Never! My father. And then the men he sold me to...I never had a chance to even think about controlling my own affairs. I never stopped to think about what I wanted. Except for one thing: I knew I never wanted to be with another man as long as I lived."

"I understand that," he said. "You told me—"

"Let me finish." She gestured with her hand at the ruins which surrounded them. "I feel like a prisoner here. I feel totally oppressed, and I'm surprised that you and the others don't feel it. It's like a real presence here, hanging over us. I *feel* it, Varian, and it makes me think of what's happened to me. What's happened to my life." She paused to rub her eyes, shake her head slowly.

"Go on...." He touched her shoulder and she pulled away.

"It's just that...I've had time to think about a lot of things since we've started the journey, and—"

"And you've decided you don't want to be with me?

That's all right, Tessa. I can understand that. That wasn't one of the conditions of saving your life...."

Tessa smiled. "No, no! It's nothing like that. No, Varian. And your saying that just proves to me again that you are a real man, a real person. I've met so few *real* people... but no, that's not what I meant."

"You're confusing me."

"It's this search," she said slowly, not looking at him. "It could go on for *years!* When I think about that, I could go crazy. I don't think I want to spend that much of my new freedom doing this, but..."

"Don't you realize what it could mean to us if we ever found the Guardian?"

"Oh yes, of course. That's not what I mean. Oh, Varian, you don't understand, do you?"

He could only shake his head. He wished that women could be more direct, more objective when discussing their own feelings.

"What I mean, Varian, is that I don't want to be with those other men. I don't want to be with *anybody* but you. You've given me my freedom and I want to share it with you."

He was tempted to say: *Is that all that's bothering you?* But he did not. He was both relieved and upset by her words. He wanted to take her in his arms and hold her warmth against his chest, but he did not do this either.

Staring into her eyes, he spoke softly: "I think I understand you, but I don't know what to do. I mean, we are *here;* we are far, far from civilization. We cannot leave here now."

"I know that," she said.

"Then what do you want me to say?"

"I don't know. If I were more of a romantic, I would tell you to say that you love me... but, I don't know what 'love' is, and I guess it would be unfair of me to ask under such circumstances."

"Well, I *am* a bit of a romantic, and I *do* think I love you, but that's not what I meant either. You know that

92

we can't leave here without Stoor and Raim, and they won't leave until they are convinced that the Guardian is not here."

"I know that."

"Then what? What do you want me to say?"

"I don't know. Tell me, do you know where we will go from here if we find nothing?"

"The Baadghizi Vale, I'd suppose. Why?"

"Is there anything in between. Any cities?"

Varian considered the question. "There's the eastern end of G'Rdellia. No big cities, but some small ones, I'm sure. We're off the established trade routes, you know."

Tessa nodded. "Do you think we might stop somewhere in G'Rdellia?"

"Maybe. I'm sure we could discuss it with Stoor, even convince him to do so. Why?"

"You *know* why." She looked at him with intense green eyes.

"Yes, I suppose I do."

"Well?"

"I don't know, Tessa. I don't know. You're asking me to choose between two things that I'm not sure I can choose between."

She looked away, up to the crisp, bright sky.

"At least you are honest about what you feel, what you think. I've never known any men that would do *that,* either."

"Let me think about it," he said weakly.

"What's the fascination here, Varian?" She looked out at the dark shapes around them.

He paused and stared at the shadowy things from the past. "I don't know. I really don't know. Just *knowing* that there were people before us, that all that we've done has been done before . . . I don't know, it *does* something to me." He drew a breath, and looked at her. "I don't have the words, Tessa. But I feel it. I'm a simple man, I know that. But there's something inside me. Something like a glowing coal that won't burn out. I need to *know!* There has to be more to the World than what we see...."

He stepped back and gestured at the sky. "Look. Look up there. Some astronomers think that each star is like the sun. Big or bigger. Can you imagine then? Can you imagine what that means? That there might be worlds like ours around all those stars. I think the the First Age knew that. I think that's where they've gone if they didn't kill each other off.

"Don't you see? I want to *know!* And I've stumbled upon something that might give me the answers."

"Might, Varian.... You don't know for certain."

"We don't *anything* for certain!" He turned away from her to stare up at the sky. "Damn it all! You want me to give up the search, don't you? You want to pack it in if there's nothing here. What would Stoor think if I just gave up and said I was going to stay in G'Rdellia?"

"Is that a threat to your masculinity?" Tessa was not smiling.

Varian laughed. "No, no! That's not what I meant at all. Think about it, Tessa. *Think* for a moment. If you were Stoor, what would you think? Your partner in a search for what might be the most priceless discovery in the history of the World suddenly decides that he wants to pull out.... Does that make sense? No, of course not! So what is the reason, thinks Stoor, and he comes up with the only viable answer: treachery."

"Do you actually think that Stoor would suspect you of—?"

Varian laughed. "I don't think it; I'm convinced."

"But why? How?"

"Because that's the kind of world it *is!* I would suspect the same thing of him if he suddenly wanted out. It's simple. You just don't walk away from a fortune! Not in this world." Varian's hands were shaking and his voice had grown loud. He turned away from her, at the same time hoping that neither of his partners at the campsite had heard him.

94

"And...and I have asked you to do that, haven't I? Asked you to walk away from a lifetime of fame and wealth...for what? For love? Oh, Varian, I don't even know what love is, so how can I ask you to give up a life's dream for it?"

Turning, he looked into her green eyes. "I don't know. How can you?"

"And how can you not hate me for forcing you to make such a choice?"

"*Hate* you? Why should I hate you?"

"Look what I'm doing to you!" She was close to tears.

Varian clearly did not understand her; she was a compelling blend of emotions and rational thoughts which would forever be a mystery to him. He needed that kind of woman.

"But that doesn't explain why I would suddenly *hate* you...."

Tessa dropped her hands to her sides in a gesture of exasperation.

"Oh! You men are impossible sometimes! Why can't you be more like women? Why can't you ever understand?"

"*I* do understand. You don't want to spend all of your time with me *and* a couple of hard-edged nomads. You want some of the comforts you tasted in Eleusynnia... and you want it with *me*, right? I understand that. And you don't want it maybe in a few years, or even longer than that, while we look for the Guardian. You want it as soon as possible. Am I right?"

She looked at him, trying to smile, or trying *not* to smile. He could not tell which "Yes, that's right." She looked down for a moment, then back at him. "And you don't hate me, or resent me, for wanting that?"

Varian laughed. "No, of course not. Perfectly understandable for a woman to feel like that."

"I resent the distinction."

Varian shrugged. "Nevertheless, the distinctions are real enough. I've never known *any* man who would feel like you do...."

"All right then...Varian?"

"What?"

"Will you just promise me one thing then?"

"Name it."

"If you understand how I feel, if you really understand, then will you promise me to think about it seriously?"

He looked at her, trying to divine what she actually meant. "Think about what? About quitting the whole thing and bagging off to G'Rdellia?"

Tessa nodded after a brief hesitation.

"Yes, of course. Of course I'll think about it...."

She smiled and put her arms around him. "Thank you," she said. "Thank you very much. You've made me very happy."

"I *have?*"

"Yes, but...you wouldn't understand."

"That's what you said before," he said, holding her in his arms. "Sure you don't want to try me?"

Tessa nodded. "I'm sure. Let's just leave it at that, all right?"

Varian shrugged. "All right....Are you sure there isn't anything else you want me to do?"

Tessa grinned. "Yes, there's *one* thing...."

And this time, Varian did understand, very well indeed.

SIX

Three and a half weeks passed before they found the Guardian.

Actually, it was the Finder which first located the ancient complex, and then it was only a vaguely defined area of electromagnetic activity. The group could not be certain it was the Citadel of the Guardian until they were finally within its fortifications, which was an accomplishment in itself.

On a map, the location was in the eastern end of the Ironfields, angling northeasterly to the Carrington Range, which formed the southern borders of the Baadghizi Vale.

Stoor was elated, so much so that he could not think of anything other than homing in on the incoming signals and reaching their origin. This meant a respite from the unending parade of tall tales. Varian was now convinced that Stoor would have had to be several hundred years old to have accomplished even half of the exploits he claimed.

The personnel carrier continued to perform flawlessly, running on the methane converter and the human-excrement fuel. The solar panel/batteries provided warmth and power for their equipment. The machine was a testament to the ingenuity and skill of the First Age, but the group knew that the vehicle was like a child's toy when contrasted with the miracles of the Guardian's Citadel, of which the robot, Kartaphilos, had been an impressive example.

Varian had been reluctant to question Tessa on her true feelings about the discovery of the Citadel's location. Whatever she felt, she masked it beneath a placid and determined demeanor, which belied only a desire to help accomplish the task at hand.

And so they mapped out a course through the ruins of the Ironfields, confident that they were closing in on the quarry. Varian had made the observation during the almost full moon cycle spent in the Ironfields that more than one great battle had been fought here. It seemed that there had been some great explosions or other cataclysmic events that had taken place in the 'fields which uncovered levels beneath the present one. Sometimes they would rumble into an area where the broken pieces of the First Age were less prevalent, where there were slashes ripped into the semidesert, revealing marbled striping of past strata. In some of these places, the bones of men were so thickly impregnated into the rock as to resemble a white thicket of brambles. Had they been mass graves? Execution areas? The remains of a singular kind of battle which could only be imagined in the blackest nightmare? It was a mystery to be forever lost, they feared, one which led only further into the shadows of other mysteries.

As they grew closer and closer to the signal source, they found other odd things. Lying among the rusting hulks of war, amidst the wind-strewn bones of men, were the bones of *other* creatures. Although there were few skeletons in relatively intact positions, the group was able to estimate the sizes of these creatures, and they were truly immense. Many of them were bipedal, possessing thighbones as thick as a man's waist and almost three ems in length. One spinal column found snaking across the sand was more than sixteen ems long! Even if this included some kind of long balancing tail, the creature would have been an impossibly huge animal, towering above men by a full ten ems. In many cases, the scorched skeletons of the large creatures were scattered in certain areas, as if burned down by some kind of immense heat. The imagination reeled when trying to conjure with the horrors which had once stalked this battleplain.

As the kays ticked past, and the atmosphere grew thick with anticipation, the hour approached when visual contact could be made. There was less than half a sun still above the littered horizon, when they saw the oddly shaped structure slowly taking form out of the haze and shifting air of convection currents.

At first it seemed to be moving, wavering, changing shape even as they stared, but this proved to be only an illusion, a trick of the climate, and perhaps their excited minds. As they drew closer, the shape attained rock-hard stability, rising up almost defiantly. It was a multitiered building of perhaps five distinct levels, although the geometry of the design could have easily disguised two or three additional levels. Having the same basic ocher color as the sand of the terrain, the structure was partially camouflaged, and they were not aware of the extremity of its architecture until they were very close. It was a maze of impossible angles, cantilevers, facings, declinations. There existed nothing like it in the known World; it climbed boldly into the sky, a symbol of the power and imagination of those who had created it.

The indicators of the Finder danced wildly, homing in on the building. There was no doubt: whatever the thing was, it was still functioning within its multifaceted walls. If the personnel carrier had been equipped with an operable radio, it would have by this time intercepted a broad-spectrum-warning broadcast from the Citadel, instructing the unauthorized vehicle to stop, identify itself, and await further instructions.

Since this was impossible, the personnel carrier would receive a different kind of greeting.

"Losin' power on the engine," said Stoor, throwing

switches, trying to locate the problem. "Lights goin' down in the console, too. Damn thing's dyin' out on us."

Varian was not listening. He had just seen movement near the base of the Citadel, which was now less than two kays distance from them.

"Look, out there. Something's coming this way."

A dark shape, not very large, but moving very fast, was homing in on them, leaving a dust-devil plume in its wake.

Without speaking, everyone reached for their weapons and trained them on the approaching vehicle, which was recognizable as such because of the large balloon tires now visible. The tires were as high as the vehicle itself.

It rolled to a quick stop very close to the personnel carrier, apparently oblivious to the weapons trained upon it. It was quite small and did not appear large enough to carry a man. There were no apparent weapons emerging from it, and for a long moment, the machine and the men stared mutely at one another.

Suddenly a stream of unrecognizable words poured forth from a speaker hidden somewhere on the surface of the small, wheeled robot. After a short pause, the message was repeated, but this time in a different language, which Varian thought might be G'Rdellian. Another pause, and it spoke again, this time in Nesporan, which everyone understood. Tessa was to later admit that she could pick up sense from all three, but was too stunned to respond, having never imagined a machine capable of speaking to someone.

"You are requested to identify yourselves immediately. You did not acknowledge the warning radio transmission, therefore a null-power net has been thrown over your vehicle."

"What's it mean?" asked Stoor. *"That* little thing has shut down our carrier?"

"It seems so," said Varian. "Let's try and do what it says."

Stoor looked from the small robot to Varian and

back, then he nodded. "We come lookin' for Cartor Fillus, or Kartaphilos, or whatever he calls himself."

"Cartor Fillus? You know of him? Please identify yourselves. Immediately."

"I'm Stoor of Hadaan. The others are Varian Hamer, Tessa of Prend, and Raim of the Maaradin."

There was a short silence, in which Varian grew cautious and a bit suspicious. His hand tensed on his sidearm, aiming it from his hip at the machine's center.

"You have been sent here by Cartor Fillus?"

"Yes," said Varian. "He told us to seek out *the Guardian.*"

"Describe Cartor Fillus, in detail."

"*Describe* him!? What in Krell's name for!?" Stoor's face was growing flush, and his hand shook as he retained his aim upon the small, dispassionate robot.

"Do as it says," said Tessa. "It's the only way the Guardian has of knowing if we're telling the truth."

Varian agreed, looked to Stoor for the go-ahead, then described the old man he had met as Kartaphilos.

Another pause, after he had completed his description, then: *"An accurate portrait. Power will be restored to your vehicle momentarily. You will follow closely behind me. Do not, at any time, deviate from the course I run. To do so may prove dangerous since this area is carefully defended against intruders."*

The little robot turned smoothly in a tight radius and began trundling back toward the dreamscape architecture of the Citadel. With a surge of power, the engine sparked alive and the lights of the control console winked on; the personnel carrier was rumbling forward as Stoor took over the controls.

Following the robot, everyone noted that there was little, if any, debris within the tight perimeter of the Citadel. It was as though the Guardian had taken measures to keep the area free of any wreckage which might prove good cover or protection to an attacking force. Clearly, anything that approached the Citadel would be totally exposed and defenseless. Looking up

at the maze of intersecting lines and angles that formed
the front face of the Citadel, Varian tried to spot any
projections, ramparts, or other signs of battlements, or
worse, any weapons which might be trained upon their
approaching vehicle. He could see nothing but the ever-
present facing of what looked like sandstone. Since it
was unlikely that the Citadel lacked this kind of defensive system, Varian concluded that the design of the
structure and the artful use of camouflage would keep
the system a secret to him.

They rolled slowly across the sand, covering the last
two kays with extreme caution. The small, wheeled
robot sat silently waiting for them as they neared what
appeared to be a seamless wall at the southern base of
the Citadel. It was then that Varian truly appreciated
the immense size of the Citadel—the wall which they
now fronted was easily 1,000 ems in length, larger even
than the Great Library at Voluspa, the most massive
building in the modern World.

A small device which looked like a deeply concave
dish rose up from the robot on a stalk and pointed at
the blank wall, and as if by magic, a rectangular seam
appeared in the sandstone, which then began shimmering a bright blue-green. The shimmering stopped,
revealing a black rectangular opening a full three ems
wide and almost five high. The little robot retracted its
dish and stalk, began rolling forward into the wall, and
was lost in the consuming darkness. Stoor hesitated for
a moment, then thrust forward on the controls. The
carrier followed its guide into the Citadel.

Once inside, they were on a smooth, featureless ramp
of dull metal, which gradually sloped downward, the
angle of descent barely perceptible. Varian looked back
to see that their entrance was sealed and invisible. If
they wanted to get out of this place, it would be impossible to go back the way they had come. But, of
course, he thought, there must be more than one exit.
There *had* to be.

Studying the area ahead, it was obvious that they

were traveling down a large corridor, illuminated by an unseen source. There were no torches, gas lamps, or lanterns, yet there was an abundance of light, as if the walls themselves were the illumination. The walls of the corridor were also featureless, although Varian imagined that this too was an illusion after seeing how the outside entrance had operated. His mind flashed back to the face of the old man/robot who had grabbed his arm on board *The Courtesan*, and told him the story of the Guardian. Oddly, Varian trusted the robot—if one could actually place trust in a machine—and believed that the story of the Guardian was true.

No one spoke during the journey downward as if everyone preferred to keep their thoughts to themselves. Or perhaps, thought Varian, it was simply fear which kept anyone from talking.

They kept moving in a slightly declined position for what seemed like an hour. It was impossible to estimate how far into the depths of the Citadel they had traveled, but Varian had the impression that it was very far indeed. It was also impossible to estimate the size of the Citadel, although there was little doubt that the First Age structure was truly immense and probably contained treasures and technological wonders far beyond the wildest imaginings of even old Stoor.

Eventually, the little robot guided them into a large five-sided room, from which several large baylike doors exited from each wall panel. The room was empty of fixtures except for a highly detailed mosaic floor, using the pentagon-shaped figure as the basic motif. There were graphics on the walls in the form of letters, and words of a language which none of the group recognized but which was presumed to be Genonese. The words could have been routing signs, warnings, or other similar instructions; it was not certain.

"You will wait here until the Guardian contacts you," said the small robot, abruptly turning and rolling off silently through one of the exits and quickly vanishing

beyond a maze of turns and switchbacks in the maze of hallways.

Stoor jumped from the cab and approached the metallic surfaces of the walls. "Just look at this workmanship, will you?"

Raim joined him, holding his scope-rifle at his hip, ever vigilant to protect his master.

"The tilework is also beautiful," said Tessa, climbing down from the cab with Varian. "Look at the patterns."

"There's no doubt about this, lad. First Age! Look! The men who control this place control the World!"

Varian was about to speak when a voice was heard behind them.

"Welcome to the Citadel. I am Guardian."

The voice was deep, masculine, full of resonance. The group wheeled about quickly to see a tall gray-haired man wearing what appeared to be a military uniform. It was a light tan color, with olive-green piping and trim. It fit the body in trim fashion, accented by brown boots and a matching weapons belt, even though the man was unarmed. His face was angular, clean-shaven, handsome. His eyes were large and brown, partially closed by heavy lids which gave him a patient, kindly appearance. His nose was sharp and hawkish, his mouth thin-lipped and forming a small grin. He had his right hand extended in the universal offering of friendship.

"Guardian?" said Stoor. "It's supposed to be a machine."

The gray-haired man smiled and stepped a few cens closer. "It is Guardian who speaks to you. What you see is only a mobile extension of myself. It is an artfully constructed robot. The physical presence of Guardian is all around you. My components are laced throughout the Citadel complex."

"Then why the robot?" asked Stoor.

"You are Stoor?" asked Guardian.

"Yeah, that's right. Now listen, aren't you goin' to answer my question?"

"Of course. The use of the humanlike robots, or *homologs* as they were once called, is a psychological technique. It was discovered long ago that members of the enclave were more disposed to deal with a machine which appeared to be human than a machine which appeared as a machine. It is more psychologically reassuring to speak with a homolog than a console of switches and LEDs. Don't you agree?"

"Not havin' ever done much of any of it, I couldn't tell you," Stoor said.

The homolog smiled. "I will meet the rest of your group, please. Simply raise your hands as your names are called. Raim. Tessa. And you are of course, then, Varian."

"Yes, I am." Varian reached and shook hands with the robot. There was no way to discern that the thing was not human. Its grip was firm, warm, decisive. "Tell me, please. Are we the first to have found you? The first since...the War?"

"The War? Oh yes, the War." The homolog's smile was replaced by a serious expression which suggested it was carefully considering an answer.

Varian watched the machine, wondering if it was so ingenious, as to reflect the thinking processes of its master-computer intelligence, or was it simply an artfully conceived diversion, a mask, under which the true intentions of the Artificial Intelligence, the Guardian, resided?

"Yes," the homolog continued. "Yes, you are the first, the *only* humans to have ever come this far."

"You mean others have found the Citadel?" asked Tessa.

"Others have stumbled upon it. Nomads and other simple types, who were unable to comprehend its significance. No, you are the first to have come bearing the words of Kartaphilos, the first to have been admitted. And I must say that although it has been a long, long time, I am most happy to receive you."

Varian smiled. "I'm afraid we did not arrive in time

to provide reinforcement...uh, the needs which sent out your messenger in the first place. I take it that you fared all right, anyway?"

The homolog smiled graciously and nodded. "Oh yes...the Citadel was preserved nicely, as you can see...."

"Actually," said Stoor, "we haven't seen much. Just a lot of empty walls. Not very exciting, you know."

"You will be given a most impressive tour, I assure you. And I apologize for the less-than-inspiring entrance, but it was the only way to accommodate your vehicle and the supplies which I assumed you would be carrying."

"Yes, we did have some things on board that we would want to hold on to. Thank you." Varian spoke the words offhandedly, wondering if the Guardian would pick up on the oblique reference to the weapons which Stoor and Raim openly brandished.

"You are more than welcome. And now, if you would please follow me, I would like to provide you with accommodations the likes of which I am sure you have never dreamed."

The homolog turned and indicated an exit leading to an illuminated corridor. Everyone gathered up a few small possessions, including their weapons, and followed. They were led a short distance to another set of doors which, at the homolog's approach, opened into a small room. Stoor hesitated in entering, until the robot explained the workings of the elevator, a common conveyance in First Age structures. Thus reassured, the party entered the device and rode it upward past uncountable levels.

When the doors reopened, even Stoor was not prepared for the sight which awaited them. They stepped out into a lush, tropical place, a bright green rain forest, a jungle of verdant plants and trees. The air was warm, humid, and heavily scented with natural perfumes of blossoms which peppered the gardens in front of them like the errant colors of an artist's palette. There was nothing so vivid, so teeming with vibrant, green life in all the known World. It was such a contrast from the harsh, desiccated world of their travels that the senses of the group were momentarily overwhelmed.

"One of the botanical gardens," said the robot. "There is at least one garden or arboretum on each level. This way, please."

They followed the robot up an inclined, railed ramp that snaked out above and sometimes through the incredible growth which literally filled the enormous chamber. At first they had not noticed it, but the air itself was alive: the steady thrumming of insects, the chirruping, and wing flapping of birds, the fluted, shrill notes of songbirds, and the splitting cries of predators.

"The Citadel served as the Nucleus for the city which once surrounded this structure. It was an agora, a forum, a marketplace for economics, for intellectual and cultural exchange." The robot gestured with his hand as he led the party through the gardens. "When the War broke out, the Nucleus of each city was transformed into a central coordinating unit for the city's defensive systems. Each one was outfitted with a special AI Series called Guardian."

"What's an AI Series?" asked Varian.

"You are speaking with one," said the robot. "AI, of course, stands for Artificial Intelligence. The series designated the type of computer specified for the task. In this case, it was called a Series IV."

"Where are all the people?" Tessa looked about the gardens like a child in a fantasyscape from fragile dreams. "What happened to everybody?"

"They are...are all gone," said the robot, as if picking its words carefully. "They have been gone for a very long time."

"Gone?" said Stoor. "You mean *dead,* don't you?"

"Yes, *dead* is the proper term." The robot reached the end of an intersection of ramps and turned right. "This way, please."

"But how did all this survive if the people were killed?" asked Varian.

Turning, the robot looked at him calmly. "It is a long story, which I will relate in detail after we have found acceptable accommodations and prepared you something to eat. Food and rest. These are primary directives for humans, am I not correct?"

"You bet your ass," said Stoor, laughing at the robot's language.

"Very well, then. I will see that you are attended. There will be plenty of time for history lessons. This way, please."

They were led down a well-illuminated corridor, whose walls were covered with impressionistic and surreal artwork. The use of color and balance and composition was in extremely good taste, so good, in fact, that it was far beyond the visitors' powers of appreciation. There were five objets d'art per wall panel, each expertly positioned.

The party was stopped in front of a door. "This is the first room," said the robot. "Since I know nothing of your sleeping/living customs, or sexual-partner preferences, I am afraid I must ask *how* you want the accommodations to be assigned."

Stoor looked at the others and grinned impishly. "How big are the rooms?" he asked.

"You would like one room for all of you?" asked the robot.

Tessa laughed. "Gods, no! Anything but that!"

"No," said Stoor. "You see, my mute friend here, Raim...he's my bodyguard. I saved his life once and he is bound by his Maaradin culture to stay with me the rest of my life. He even sleeps with me, *but*"—Stoor held up his hand, grinning through his beard—"he don't sleep *with* me, if you can feature what I mean?"

Varian smiled and the robot deadpanned an affirmative reply, indicating that Raim and Stoor could take the room behind the door. He placed Stoor's palm against a small black plate by the door and the plate flashed strobically white. He repeated the procedure with Raim's hand, illustrating the workings of a palm-print lock.

When the old man and his friend had entered the room, the robot led Varian and Tessa to the next door on the same side of the corridor. "Will you two also be sharing a room?"

"Yes," said Tessa. She would not look at Varian who was smiling broadly at her shyness, which had survived despite the abasing trauma of her younger days.

They entered the room, after palm-printing the lock, and saw that it possessed five walls in the shape of a pentagon. Each wall seemed to glow with a soft illumination, each with a different but complementary color. The scheme of colors were combined with earth tones: pastel yellows, oranges, browns, bone-whites...On the far wall, covering most of the panel hung a large black pane, which appeared to consist of the same material as the palm-print lock. The robot gestured about the room pointing to a platform which was obviously a bed, although it was located atop a small ziggurat rather than a simple pallet. The robot explained that the bed was filled with a gelatin-like substance, actually a lab-cultured, semiorganic material which would naturally conform to the shape of the person who reclined upon it. A plant-animal hybrid, the substance provided a maximum of sleeping or recreational comfort, or so said the robot. The homolog also demonstrated the use of the bath and toilet facilities, based upon principles which were effective if not easily comprehended. The screen on the distant wall, when switched on, provided a spectacular view of the lands surrounding the Citadel, including the Carrington Range, which spiked the distant horizon with snow-flecked peaks.

It was a room crammed with devices, ideas, and materials of another age. It was a conscious attempt to create warmth and comfort and security, but to Varian, there seemed to be something absent. There was a coldness which pervaded the room like a living presence, an artificiality to which Varian knew he could never grow accustomed. He could not articulate his feelings other than to mentally remark upon the totally antiseptic quality of the room, of the Citadel in general. There was no dust—no traces of life upon anything. Not a fingerprint, a smear, the slightest sign of anything out of place.

They were also given a full complement of clothes of the same basic design and cut as the robot's—informal, semimilitary, functional, and comfortable. After this, they were led to a small dining area which overlooked the botanical gardens. Everything was served, and presumably prepared, by the Guardian's homolog, and the party felt as if they were being feted in the court of a generous, if somewhat eccentric, king.

There were many questions to be asked, and the group attempted to pass the dinner period in a running conversation with the Guardian. It was odd, then, that so many of their queries were evaded skillfully and at times quite bluntly not answered. For instance, the Guardian claimed to be unaware of how much time had passed since the War, to have no idea *when* the First Age came to its end, or even how the event took place. It also claimed to be ignorant of the vastness of the Ironfields or the confusing strata of wreckage which suggested a multiplicity of wars over the millennia.

Varian and Stoor began to lose patience with the homolog, who fielded each question with a facility that was both glib and insulting.

"Surely there must be some kind of library here," said Varian. "A place where the people went to seek information...."

"Of course," said the homolog. "There is a Data Retrieval Center and many access terminals throughout the complex. To use them, you simply punch in your request on the keyboard or use the vocal-register inputs."

"Aren't these things connected to main machinery?"

asked Stoor. "Aren't they all part of the same system? That is...*you?* The Guardian?"

"Yes, that is also true."

"Then we shouldn't have to use a terminal," said Tessa. "We should be able to simply ask *you!*"

"This is also correct."

"But you claim you don't know a whole lot of what we ask you," said Stoor. "So it don't matter whether we ask the terminals or not...we'll get the same answers as we'd get from *you.*"

"This is also correct." The homolog smiled.

There was an awkward silence at the table. All four members of the group stared at the robot who stood at the far end. It had an implacable expression on its face, despite the attempt to appear congenial. No longer was the robot's face one of a kindly, even grandfatherly, type. It was the face of a cold, calculating *presence*, which now seemed to be dispensing with all efforts to mask its true nature.

"Let me ask you something else?" said Varian.

"Of course. Anything."

"I doubt *that*," said Tessa.

"Tessa, wait," Varian said. "Listen, when I spoke with Kartaphilos, the robot said he was seeking out people who were bright enough to find this place, to assist the Guardian in some way. Is that correct?"

"Oh yes," said the robot. "That is correct."

"What kind of assistance, then? What do you want from us?"

"Many things, Varian Hamer. And they will be made clear to you in due time. *All* your questions will be answered *in due time.*"

"You speak as if you have things worked out on a schedule, a timetable."

The robot nodded slowly. "You are correct again."

Varian shook his head, let his hand rest easily on his sidearm. It was not meant as a threatening gesture, but was merely an unconscious defensive movement.

"Tell me something else," he said. "You know more than you are telling us.... I'm sure of it. But why?"

"I cannot explain that now, other than to say you are again correct. Kartaphilos was a wise judge of humans. I must compliment him."

"He's here?" asked Stoor.

"Not yet, but he has been...how would you say it?...recalled from active duty? Yes, he has been recalled. He will arrive eventually."

"Wait a second!" said Stoor, pounding a fist upon the table. "Varian's right. Somethin' the Krell's goin' on here and I want to know what it is. Somethin' *stinks* around here!

"The air is climatically controlled. There are no odors present which should be noisome to humans."

"Shit, will you listen to him?" said Stoor, grinning in spite of his irritation.

"We were led to believe that the Guardian was *servant* of humankind," said Varian. "...that we would be given the secrets of the First Age if we were ever to find this place."

"And that the World would benefit from the knowledge that's obviously contained here..." said Tessa.

The homolog nodded slowly again. Its smile was still fixed inanely upon its face like a mask of brittle construction. "Those are definite possibilities which may derive from your discovery of the Citadel, that is correct. But before that can happen, there are certain... events...which must take place."

"Events?" said Stoor in a voice that was slightly less than a bellow. "What kind of *events?*"

"You will understand them as they are taking place. That is all I can tell you now."

Tessa stood up from her seat and faced the homolog. "Guardian, please tell me I'm wrong, but you speak as if...as if we're prisoners here."

There was another awkward moment of silence. The eyes of the group were all upon the homolog, which returned their stares with eyes of dark determination.

"You are not wrong," it said finally.

SEVEN

Very soon after this, the illusions began.

At least, everyone *hoped* they were illusions. Otherwise, it was madness.

Varian had been walking alone through the third level of the Citadel. Here were the vast Works of the place: machine shops, foundries, mills, power plants, a matrix of factory operations which would have been able to recontour an entire country in the modern World. It was a miniature city of precision machinery—glinting steel, mirrored alloys, massive turbines, and lathes and die cutters. And all as silent as the grave. There was not a sound within the great emptiness of the Works. No man walked; no one touched the fine controls; the immense furnaces and converters lay cool and dead.

Because there were no people. One of Guardian's unanswerable—or rather, unanswered—questions. It was the largest question in Varian's mind: Where had they gone? Was it actually possible that the War had killed them off so totally? Were they kept prisoner in some hidden part of the Citadel? Was the Guardian a machine gone mad? If so, how would he, or any of the group, ever move against it?

They lacked the power or, more important, the understanding to cope with Guardian on its own terms. Every instant he was being reminded of the advanced minds which conceived the place where he now walked. They would be fools to think they could match wits or plans with even the stepchildren of such a society.

He continued walking, his weapons belt hanging limply over his Citadel "uniform." He, as all the others, had been allowed to carry their weapons with them; it was an apparent move on Guardian's part to show that it had nothing to fear from them. Leaving the Works, he turned a corner and entered a large mall where there had once been throngs of people, meeting and interacting in an open forum. It was now a placid park, a slice of green, accented by trees the likes of which Varian had never known existed on Earth.

As he crossed expertly manicured lawns, he sensed movement from the corner of his eye. Wheeling rapidly on the balls of his feet and pulling out his sidearm in one quick motion—as old Furioso had taught him years ago—he leveled the weapon at three standing figures grouped gracefully under a copse of autumn-flecked trees.

Three beautiful women. Standing amidst the trees, looking very composed, as if they expected him.

"Good afternoon, sir," said one of the women. "I am Hera." She was the tallest of the three, with blue-green eyes and auburn hair of great length, depth, and sheen. Her face was angular, her smile enchanting. She was a beautiful woman. She wore a long, extremely sheer gown, through which he could see her body—muscled, yet lithe and well proportioned.

"I am Varian Hamer," he said, lowering his weapon, yet not putting it away. "What are you doing here?...I mean, I thought I was alone here...."

"That is no matter," said Hera. "We are here only to ask you a small favor." Hera indicated her two companions, who now stepped forward and demurely bowed their heads, dropping their gaze for a moment. "This is Athena, and this is Aphrodite."

Varian bowed to the ladies, studying them quickly. Athena had hair as dark as a raven, and moody features: almond eyes of brown, well-tanned complexion, full, sensuous mouth, and an aquiline nose. Her cheekbones were high and prominent. She wore a diaphanous gown similar to Hera's, through which her flowing hips and large-nippled breasts were very evident. Aphrodite, though no less stunning in appearance, was quite different: golden-blond hair, sky-blue eyes and long lashes, pert and tiny nose, a small, delicate mouth, gently curved like an archer's bow. She too wore the revealing gown of the first two women and was no less physically endowed. In fact, Varian could not recall ever seeing three women together who were such perfect, but different, examples of feminine beauty.

"We have a problem," said the one called Athena.

"Yes," said Aphrodite. "We were at a banquet for a few friends of ours..."

Varian wanted to interrupt them, to ask from where they came, *whose* banquet, by what means had they come here...? But he could say nothing. It was as though they were exerting some influence over him.

"And there was a special delivery," said Hera, reaching into the folds of her gown, producing an exquisite piece of sculpture—a golden apple. Varian, being the perceptive observer that he was, was as much entranced by the perfection of the golden sculpture as he was by Hera's seeming magic: she had been carrying that apple *somewhere* in her gown, but it was so sheer, and filmy, and clinging...where had she hidden it?

"Special delivery?" he finally said.

"Yes," said Athena, her dark hair falling sensuously across her face. "It was left with a small message attached which instructed the piece to be given to the most beautiful woman at the banquet."

"Actually," said Aphrodite, "it read *for the Fairest,* and everyone vied for its possession, until the choice was narrowed down to us three."

"I'm afraid I don't understand all this," said Varian, still clutching his sidearm. He was reluctant to put it away, since he quite frankly did not trust the women's story, and suspected them of being several of the Guardian's homologs. "Could you please tell me what banquet this was, and where you have come from? I was not expecting anyone else to be here, you see...."

Hera smiled. "It is the banquet of King Peleus and Thetis. It was held on Olympus, of course. Now, please, we have not much time and we wish your help."

"Yes, we do," said Athena and Aphrodite together.

Varian was confused and somehow intimidated by the women. He had never heard of the King, his companion, nor Olympus, but his mind was not focusing on these things. He found himself hanging on Hera's last words, that they needed his help. "What can I do for you?"

"It's fairly obvious, isn't?" asked Athena. "We want you to be the judge. We want you to choose which one of us is the most beautiful...."

"That's correct," said the other two.

Something reeled in his mind. The thought of choosing between the three women was almost inconceivable, and he wondered if he was at all capable of it. Each one, in her own way, was so singularly exotic, mysteriously attractive...it was not a choice any man would anticipate.

"I don't know if I can do it."

"Oh, you can do it," said Athena.

"But you will probably need some time to think about it," said Aphrodite. "We understand that."

"And so," said Athena, "we shall leave you for a while, then return for your decision."

Before Varian could object, all three women turned and glided quickly through a break in the grove of trees. He jumped to follow, to catch up with them, and found that they had vanished completely. There was no sound, no evidence of their ever having been there. He was a man who had fought duels, ambushes, taken part in sea raids and other military actions, but he had never felt the cold bolt of fear that now shot through him.

There was a sound behind him.

Whirling quickly, he turned to face the enigmatic Hera, standing alone before him. She smiled at him coyly, her auburn hair falling naturally about her shoulders.

"Don't be alarmed," she said. "I've come to offer you a bargain."

"What?" Varian was very confused now.

"It's quite simple, really. If you choose *me*, I am prepared to give you political control of the entire World. Don't ask how I can do it, just believe me when I say that I can. Simple, see? Pick me, and you are the Emperor of the World."

"It's not possible.... You—"

"I am serious," said Hera, and her voice cut through him like a blade. She carried the authority and haughty bearing of someone who was accustomed to power and its many uses. For some reason, unexplainable at the time, Varian believed her.

"I will have to consider it," said Varian.

"Of course." Hera smiled knowingly and walked into the forest.

Before he could follow her, to see how she effected her mysterious exit, there was another sound behind him. Someone was calling his name.

He turned and was only half surprised to see Athena, dark, sultry Athena, standing close to him, one bare leg extended through a slit in her gown and her hips canted at a provocative angle.

"I also have a bargain," she said.

"I'm somehow not surprised."

Athena laughed. It was like a series of musical notes, hypnotic and extremely pleasing. "No, Varian. Not what you may think it is."

"Go on then. If I choose you, I get what?"

"It's very simple. You will get what you came here for. The secret of the Citadel. The knowledge of the Guardian and a true history of the First Age."

His heart jumped, a physical reaction which characterized the impact the words made upon his mind. How could she know what he wanted? How could she give it to him?

"There is no questioning my ability to give you what you want," she said, as though she knew his thoughts.

"I've heard that somewhere else, I think."

"Nevertheless, you must choose."

"I'll have to think about this if you don't mind."

Athena smiled and stepped backward, blending into the lush colors of the forest. In an instant she was gone.

He was still staring at the place where she had disappeared when he heard his name once more.

Turning slowly this time, Varian was not at all surprised to see the lovely Aphrodite standing several paces away from him.

"I've been expecting you," he said, smiling sardonically.

"Have you?"

"Let's keep things short and simple. If I choose you, what do I get?"

Aphrodite giggled. "You are quite pragmatic, aren't you?"

"When the situation warrants. I feel like I am playing some kind of vast game, so I figured I should get into the spirit of the thing."

Aphrodite continued to smile as she studied him. "What have the others offered? The usual? Wealth? Power?"

"A slight variation," said Varian. "One gave a combination of the first two; the other, knowledge."

"*Knowledge!* A formidable adversary, that one," said Aphrodite.

Varian watched her. "When compared to what?" he asked.

Aphrodite touched a clasp at the neck of her gown.

"To this," she said as the gown fell away in a whispering rush. She stood naked before him and she was truly the most perfect woman he had ever seen. Her skin was ivory and flawless, smooth and supple. Her legs were long, firm; her breasts high and pointed; her stomach flat above a golden triangle equal in brilliance to the blond tresses of her head.

His blood pounded in his temples, and in other places. He struggled to retain his composure, but never had he ever beheld such a vision. Forcing the words between his teeth, he told her that he would have to consider her offer, as well as the others.

Gracefully, she stooped to gather up her gown, and grasping it to her breasts, she backed away into the foliage—a now familiar exit.

Time became an insubstantial thing. It stretched and eddied and dripped like wax about him; he was not conscious of it. He felt lost in a swirl of memories and impressions which could-have-been, but on the other hand...

He marveled at the utter unreality of the experience. The meaning of it. The incomprehensibility. The absurdity. Again the sensation of being in a game came over him, and he attempted to reconcile that, but could not. Curiously, he gave little attention to which of the three offers he would choose.

Until all three appeared once again, each one seeming to be on the verge of giving him a conspiratorial wink.

"We await your choice," said Hera.

Varian laughed. "Believe it or not, so do I."

None of them smiled, nor did they reply. It sobered him and he regarded them as dispassionately as possible under the circumstances.

"All right, let me preface my choice with a few words, which concerns the reality of this whole thing. I am a skeptic if you must know. Therefore, I doubt whether or not any of this is really happening. Under actual circumstances, I would opt for the offer of knowledge—I assume you are all aware of each other's little bargains?—especially since I find all three of you equally 'fair,' as the inscription read."

At this point, Athena's expression brightened, the

hint of a smile appeared at the corners of her full mouth.

"However," continued Varian, "I cannot make myself believe that this is more than fantasy. Although I do not like the idea of sacrificing one aspect of life for another, I realize that life is indeed a parade of choices, of denials, and sacrifices."

"Get to the point," said Hera, who seemed to realize that her offer of power was *not* going to be the chosen one.

Varian laughed. "The point is simply this. Under these peculiar circumstances, I would have to say that Aphrodite is 'the fairest' of all of you."

There was, for an instant, a total pause—in sound, in breath, in motion. Varian felt a moment of vertigo, which quickly passed, then time seemed to start up again. Aphrodite smiled and stepped forward, and for a moment he thought that it was all *real,* that she was going to—

He blinked his eyes, and it was finished.

The three women, mysteriously and stunningly beautiful, had disappeared. Vanished more quickly than smoke in a strong breeze. They were simply gone.

Although Raim never spoke, *could* never speak, he was still a man of great wit and understanding. Many evenings during their journey, he had entertained the others with his talent for mime and impersonation, and with the music he played upon the small flutelike instrument called the arthis. Its playing required the musician to have an elegant dexterity in his fingers, but also a firm control of breath and lips. The tongue must remain depressed in order to achieve proper tone; since Raim's tongue had been cut out, he was especially adept on the arthis.

It was late evening, after dinner, and the others had said their good nights, having gone to their quarters. The robot had passed through, arrogant and yet accommodating as usual, but had said nothing to Raim. The small, muscular man was feeling restless, and since he could not sleep, he attempted a walk through the levels of the Citadel.

Coming to the lowest levels in the place, he found himself surrounded by the thrumming of great machines—the purposes of which were far beyond his understanding and so he ignored them. Pausing for a rest on the edge of a catwalk spanning two large generators, Raim pulled out his arthis and began to play. The music rose above the hum of the machinery, sounding as if amplified, and echoed throughout the vast chamber. It was a pleasant acoustical effect, prompting him to play louder.

Music was very special to Raim. It was the only kind of sound he was able to create, and he treasured his ability on the arthis. He used his music to communicate his thoughts and his feelings. He poured his soul into the tiny instrument and warmed to its compassionate sounds.

It was while he played that the dark vision came to him.

Out of the shadows of the great machines a large indistinct figure drew up. It was darker than black, yet insubstantial like swirling smoke. Its face was not visible because of the full hood and cloak which covered its form and seemed to flow like a liquid.

The soft notes of a waltzlike tune died in his throat as Raim looked up to see the thing-out-of-nightmare looming over him. In an instant he jumped to his feet and flicked out his shortsword, but was paralyzed as the thing spoke to him.

"Your weapon is useless upon me.... Be still and listen."

Who are you? Raim's mind screamed out the question.

And the thing seemed to hear him. "I am Pluto," it said. A voice of infinite resonance, depth, power.

What do you want with me?

"You play well, Raim."

What do you want? Raim refused to drop his sword, still poised ready for a strike, a defensive maneuver.

"Your music is sweet, as once was Marise."

The mention of his long-dead wife pierced him like a sword's point. His arms fell to his side as he was swept up in a rush of memories: a petite, dark-eyed woman; a voice like a nightingale's; the quick fluttering gestures and movements of a fragile bird; the mirror-image of Raim's coarse ways; the perfect complement to him. He had loved her so fiercely that no woman had ever touched his heart since her terrible death so many years ago.

But how could this thing know of Marise?

He thought of his young bride and the attack upon the Maaradin; of how the secondary keep had been temporarily overrun and she had been trapped in the sweep of the invaders; of the moment when he found her broken, lifeless body in the dusty ruins of the battle; and of how he had then thrown himself at her killers, hoping only to join her in death.

"I know of Marise, musician. I am her keeper...."

Raim shuddered as he stared into the folds of the figure's hood, straining to see the hint of features hidden in the shadows. This could not be Death he encountered. There was no such thing, no such animation, except in the minds of men.

"I am quite real. And I offer you your Marise."

Marise! Marise! The thought of seeing her again filled him with a raw, irrational flood of feelings. It was a blend of panic and unrestrainable joy. All judgment, reason, fleeing under this storm of emotion.

"You may have her. You may lead her from this Underworld of death and eternal darkness...."

How? Tell me what I must do! Where is she!

"You will follow the St. Elmo's fire," said the thing, and an iridescent ball of swampfire danced in front of the figure. "*And* you will play your instrument as you have never played it."

What?

"To enter the world of the dead, you must charm the guardians and dwellers there, or you yourself shall not return. You shall follow the swampfire until you find her, playing all the time."

I will do it! I will do anything you say! His heart pounded like a blacksmith's hammer, almost bursting in his chest. In his mindless desire, he felt like a stag in a burning forest, compelled to rush onward.

"There is more. You must continue playing. You cannot speak to her until you have returned here, until you are out of my world. One more thing: you must not look back to her, once you have begun your journey from the Underworld. You must not look back until you have returned *here*. Understood?"

Raim nodded, watching the swampfire as it glided off down a dark, steel corridor which now appeared as a glazed-wall cavern in ancient rock. His hands were slippery as he brought the arthis to his lips.

The passage led into utter darkness. The cowled figure had vanished like the smoke he appeared to be. The corridors of the Citadel transformed into a bleak, downward-sloping tunnel which looked in the faint glow of the swampfire like the infinite maw of some great beast. Raim's music, a beautiful intruder, echoed through the place, assaulting the silence.

He came upon a raging creature, which appeared to be a wolf, its thickly sinewed body held to a rock by a massive chain. From its neck stretched three heads, all facing him; three pairs of eyes burning into him; the three-fanged mouths drooling in anticipation of tearing him to ribbons. But remembering the words of the one called Pluto, Raim continued to play, and the three-headed beast then ceased its savagings of the air, fell to its knees, and composed itself as if drugged by the lyrical music.

Raim was barely aware of the music, so amazed was he by the effects of its playing. He passed by the watchdog, for that was what it must have been, and entered a vast chamber, where he saw a man pushing a giant boulder up an impossible grade. The man paused to listen to Raim's music, as did likewise a man tied to a great wheel, and a hoard of others, all of whom were suffering torturous indignities of horrible devise. Raim continued to follow the swampfire, coming finally to a black river where throngs of people stood transfixed by his music on the far shore. He stood playing until he saw a boatman, a gondolier, approaching him in a flat-bottomed skiff.

Seated in the rear of the boat sat a small, dark-haired woman. *Marise!*

So shocked to see her, Raim almost paused in his playing, but fearfully remembered the words of the hooded one. With the greatest effort, he piped on as the boatman, a reed-thin, scrofulous fellow, assisted Raim's beloved wife from the boat. She moved with the familiar grace and facility which he had remembered, and his heart soared in his chest, giving rise to even more poignant, more beautiful music.

Looking quickly away, following the swampfire, Raim walked hesitantly back along the first path. He strained to hear Marise's footsteps behind him and could hear them in the odd moments when there was a natural pause in his melody, or in that breath of time when his own steps were not echoing off the cold walls of the cavern.

They passed the place of tortures and again everyone paused to watch their flight from the darkness. As Raim moved along, following the swampfire and playing his arthis, he watched the cavern walls grow lighter, changing ever so slowly, once again becoming the corridors of the Citadel. He passed the three-headed wolf, still chained to its rock, still soothed by the music.

They were almost free, almost out of the place of death. Thoughts of Marise filled him and he wanted to believe in this wild dream/adventure; he wanted to know that she was indeed following him. He had not heard her breath, her footstep, had not sensed her presence in what seemed like a long time.

Up ahead, Raim could see where the tunnel-like confines of the cavern gave way to the smoothness of the Citadel. Almost out of the place. Almost free! *Marise! Marise!* Her name filled him with excitement and he turned as he approached the beginning of the corridor, reaching back to take her hand and pull her finally to him. How he longed to hold her against his chest once more!

But it was not to be.

His lovely bride, so close behind him, extended her arms to him, but there was an expression of pain, of sadness, and defeat upon her face. Even as he touched her tiny hands, she began to fade away like frost on an autumn morning.

Marise! The thought burned in his mind as he knew he was losing her. He knew in that instant that he had turned back to her too soon, that she would be gone, and he would never see her again.

Her image was replaced by the looming figure in the dark robes, and the transformation plunged Raim into a moment of madness. Opening his mouth, he screamed...an inarticulate scream which rushed from the pit of his being and echoed through the empty steel corridors. He turned away from the shadowed thing and lost his balance. The planes and angles of the walls spun wildly across his vision, more and more rapidly, until he passed out....

On that same evening, after having retired to his room, and wondering only briefly where his companion might have wandered, old Stoor reclined on his bed, contemplating the possibilities of escaping from the place where they had so blithely entered. It was not the first time he'd been held prisoner—in a life as full as his, he could not actually recall the exact number of times—but it was easily the most mystifying.

The first rule in effecting an escape was to fully understand and truly *know* your captor. Stoor had no such knowledge, and it frustrated him. But he would

127

not give up until he discovered what made the odd Guardian tick; he *would* know his captor. He was consumed with recurring thoughts such as this, and he passed the sleepless hours by smoking his pipe and waiting for Raim.

Reclining in his bed, he was shocked to see something moving near the far wall. Standing quickly, he reached for his weapon and watched as the shimmering in the air took shape. It was a man dressed in crude armor and an odd-looking battle helmet. He carried a large spear.

"By Krell! Don't move or you're a dead man!"

The intruder laughed and eased his spear to the ground, its business end pointing to the ceiling. "I am neither dead nor alive, and your weapons would have no effect on me. I am here to make you an interesting proposition...."

"Here? How you'd *get* here's what I want to know."

"I could not explain it simply enough so that you would ever understand. It would be better if you would just accept the fact that I am indeed *here*."

Stoor shook his head. "Sorry, can't do that. I've been too stubborn and too old for too long. Now what's goin' on? I locked that door myself. You another one of them robots?"

The man laughed. "Hardly. I am Zeus."

"Who?" Stoor looked dumbly at the man, although there was something about the name which ached in his memory. Something familiar.

"I have been called by other names, but Zeus is my preference. If you must know, I walked through your wall."

"Through it, huh? Some kind of ghost, I suppose. Well, I'm afraid I don't believe in ghosts. You see I know somethin' about science *and* magic, and I'm not as ignorant as I might look. I'm no sandgrubber who's gonna think you're hot shit 'cause you got a cigarette lighter or a flashlight in your pocket."

The man laughed again. "Well, that's good to know.

I didn't feel like bothering with such gimmickery anyway."

"What you want in here?"

"I'm getting to that. Let's say that I have something that you want very much, all right?"

"Like what?"

"Like your freedom...."

The word seemed to strike a chord within Stoor's soul. He stood immobile for a moment, and his jaw dropped slightly open.

"My freedom?"

"Precisely."

"Who *are* you, anyway?"

"Let's just say that I mean what I say, and that I have some influence around here."

"You're the Guardian, aren't you?"

"No."

"Nothin' goes on here without that machine knowin' it! You must think I'm awful stupid!"

"Nevertheless, I am not Guardian. But I *can* get you out."

"What about the others?"

"Their freedom is also guaranteed, except one."

"What're you talking about? Which one. Who?"

"It's fairly well obvious that you will have to fight your way out of here.... You have considered that?" Zeus paced easily about the five-sided room.

"The thought's occurred to me."

"Good. Now let's say that I am prepared to warrant your safety and effect your escape. Even though you don't believe me, let's just say so for argument's sake. All right?"

"Go on."

"But there is one catch. You see, as Zeus, I am entitled to my idiosyncrasies...."

"Like what?"

"Like I am very fond of sacrifices."

"Of what?"

"You know, I like something, or preferably some*one,* offered up to me as a show of...say, good faith."

"Offered *up?* You sound like those primitives in the Baadghizi, the Hurrun! Do you like stone altars too?!"

Zeus shrugged. "They're not bad, but I really do require a sacrificial victim."

Stoor looked at the man and saw that despite his cavalier attitude and demeanor, his eyes were cold and hard as steel. The man was serious.

"And who did you have in mind? Anybody in particular?"

"Of course."

"Who, then?"

Zeus smiled. "At last, we reach the bargaining position. Your freedom...your freedom for the life of Raim."

"Raim! You're outta your mind! He's the only friend, the *best* friend, I've ever had. Every man should wish to have a friend like him. By Krell! He's like a son to me!" Stoor laughed nervously, but the oddly attired man called Zeus did not smile.

"Precisely, Stoor. Precisely."

"Huh?"

"In order for a sacrifice to mean anything, the item being relinquished must be of some intrinsic worth, am I not correct?"

"Some intrinsic worth? A human life? Of a friend, yet? I'd *say* it had worth!"

"Well, that is my price.... You give me Raim, and I will see that the rest of you will win your contest against Guardian, and be free of this place."

"Ridiculous. What do you want with Raim? What will you do with him?"

Zeus grinned. "Why, kill him, of course!"

Stoor almost turned away from the man, but remembered that one never turns his back on a man with a weapon. "You're insane!" He spit out the words, almost tempted to attack the man and be done with the confrontation. He could feel the resentment building in him, and he was tired of talking.

"Insane? Hardly. Think on this, Stoor: Would not Raim gladly lay down his life for you?"

"What?"

"Raim. Is he not indebted to you? Didn't you tell everyone that you saved his life long ago and that he is forever in your service because of it?"

"Yes, but—"

"Then he, in a sense, owes *you* his life. I am certain that if you asked him to sacrifice himself for the good of the others, he would comply without compunction."

"Perhaps he would... but that's his decision to make, not mine."

"Is it? You decided years ago to *save* his life. You have already exerted your control over his life or death; there is no reason to relinquish it now."

"No. It's not right!"

"There is no right or wrong. There is only what *is*. Asking Raim is only a formality. You *know* that."

"And you're askin' me to act in his place. Give the word, so to speak?"

"It is necessary that it be done that way, believe me. What we are talking about is an age-old ethical question. And its answer must be reevaluated and reanswered every time it is asked anew."

"What are you talkin' about?"

Zeus looked away, for a moment, as if remembering something. "Once a man named Agamemnon was asked to sacrifice his daughter..."

Stoor snapped up his head, staring intently at Zeus. Of course! The man's words had sprung the memory. He knew now where he had heard the name before....

"...and the daughter's name," said Stoor, "was Iphigenia!"

Now Zeus looked startled. "You know? How *could* you?"

Stoor smiled. "Only the way *I* heard it, she was killed

for somebody named Artemis. That's not one of your other names, is it?"

"No, but she is a friend of mine. We do each other favors."

"I'm sure you do."

"I am...surprised that you know of us," said Zeus, now regaining his composure. "But that does not change my request."

Stoor smiled. "I'll give you my answer, but first you'll have to level with me."

"Level?"

"Tell me the truth, all right?"

"I cannot bargain."

"Then I cannot answer," said Stoor.

A silence passed between them and Zeus grew impatient. "All right, what is it you want to know?"

"This isn't real, is it?"

"What do you mean?"

"I mean this is some kind of illusion, some kind of *game* or something, right?"

"What do you mean by that?" Zeus maintained his calm, but there was a suggestion of unease in his voice.

"I mean you aren't really prepared to give us our means of escape, just like you aren't really going to take Raim's life if I give it to you...because you don't really exist!"

Zeus grinned. "Old Stoor. You are a tough old man...."

"I'm right, then!? I'm right, ain't I?"

"In a sense."

"What in Krell's that mean?"

"That I do not have the power as you say, that this may not...be as it seems."

"Sounds like what you want more than anything is some information. Some knowledge...?"

Zeus nodded his head. "Please tell me now! What would you do? Would you make the sacrifice?"

Stoor studied the face of the one who claimed to be Zeus. There was something about the man's eyes, or

132

whatever thing it was that masqueraded as a man, something which *needed* an answer. The question was burning into him now: *Why?* What was going on here?

"Please give me your answer," said Zeus.

"All right," said Stoor. "I *would* sacrifice him...." Under certain conditions, thought Stoor. He was not a superstitious man, nor did he believe in the ancient legends, but there *was* a kernel of fact, or wisdom actually, to be found in almost all the old fables. He answered as he had, as much from curiosity to see what would come next as from his conviction that it was the correct answer.

Zeus nodded and stepped back toward the solid wall. "Thank you," he said. "Thank you very much. I will leave you now."

"Wait!" said Stoor, and the figure did pause for a moment before fading through the wall into nothingness.

Naturally, Tessa was not excluded from the series of odd encounters which befell the group. She was in the Data Retrieval chamber, trying to learn the many uses of the machines and equipment, when a strangely attired man appeared to her. He wore the armor of a primitive warrior, yet his face reflected intelligence, even cunning.

She was not certain from where he had come. It seemed that in a moment he was simply *there*. Under one arm he carried an ornately carved box of adamantine, ebony, ivory, and other exotic woods. It was a beautiful piece of craftsmanship, and even though she was startled, even frightened by the sudden appearance of the man, she found that she had difficulty taking her eyes from the box.

"Good evening, my Tessa," said the man. His voice was smooth and comforting, although quite resonant, bespeaking power and authority.

"Who are you?" she asked, not trying to hide her indignity or a small amount of fear.

"You need not be afraid of me," said the man. "I am called Zeus. You have heard of me?"

She paused for a moment, considering the question, then shook her head. It was a marvelous piece of work, she thought in spite of herself, still stealing glances at the piece which the man carried.

"You have not? Ah, that is good."

"Good?"

"You will understand everything...someday, but for now, I wish to tell you something."

"Tell me something. What are you doing here? I thought everyone had disappeared long ago. You must be from Guardian then?"

"Not exactly," was all he said and took a step closer to her.

She immediately tensed and her mind raced, trying to recall some of the basic techniques in self-defense which Varian had been teaching her. They had all seemed so simple when she was learning them, but now, when she needed the knowledge, it would not come to her.

"Is there something wrong?" asked Zeus.

"Please, don't come any closer. I don't know you....I can't...I can't trust you."

The man paused and smiled. It was a very disarming, quite charming smile, and she relaxed visibly. There was something odd about him that went beyond his strange attire and his speech, which she could not place as having any dialect patterns in the known World.

"Please, I assure you I mean no harm. I have come, in fact, to give you a gift...."

"Me? A gift?" Tessa laughed at the incongruity of the thought. It was the last thing she would have expected from the man, yet her gaze flew instantly back to the box he carried.

"But first, a story," he said, moving to the edge of a desktop, where he half sat, composing himself in a most casual fashion.

"A story? Oh yes, you said something before about that."

"Yes, I did. Now listen, please, it is a story of creation. Do you know any?"

"I have heard folktales. But they are just foolishness...."

Zeus smiled. "Yes, they *are*, aren't they?" He paused to rub his beard contemplatively and place the box on the desktop. "Now then, listen. A long time ago, when the world was being pulled together out of Chaos, there were two brothers—their names do not matter—who were very different in personality and in worth, even though both were what we would call, for want of a better word, 'gods.'"

"Gods?" Tessa looked at him oddly.

"Yes, you know—all powerful, quite influential around the universe, that sort of fellow...."

"Oh...oh yes, of course," she said, a bit patronizingly.

"Well, come now, I mean this *is* a creation tale, isn't it?" asked Zeus.

"Yes, I suppose you're right," she said. "Go on, now."

"All right. And so, these brothers were quite different types of gods. Brother Number One was very, very wise. The wisest perhaps of all the gods; and of course, Number Two—"

"Was not very bright, scatterbrained, perhaps...a real problem," said Tessa.

"Are you sure you haven't heard this one?"

Tessa smiled. "No, but it *is* rather obvious so far, isn't it?"

Zeus shrugged. "I guess so," he said. "Anyway, to continue: Both brothers had a large hand in creating the World, giving it all its animals and even mankind itself—only at first the situation was quite literal. I mean it *was* mankind. No women yet. And believe it or not, things went along rather nicely for a while, until the brothers did something (I don't remember what it was but it had something to do with offerings which the Elder—the chief deity—was to receive from men) which angered the Elder. And so, the elder god devised a unique punishment for the two brothers... he created a woman and gave her to Brother Number Two for his wife."

"That's a *punishment?*"

Again Zeus shrugged. "I didn't make it up; I can only tell it like it is...."

"Very well," she said. "What happened next?"

"Well, Brother Number One was very upset about this turn of events... not because he didn't receive the woman for a wife, but because he did not trust the elder god's apparent kindness, nor did he have much faith in his brother's competence to handle the situation. It did not, by the way, help matters that the woman was truly beautiful—the most beautiful woman who has ever lived, from now till the present. She was so magnificently created, in fact, that Brother Number Two lost all of what little judgment he might have possessed when dealing with her. The results was that the 'first' woman became a pampered, spoiled princess, who grew quickly accustomed to getting her own way in all matters. This, too, upset Brother Number One, but he busied himself with the new World, which he had created, and tried to make things as good as he could for the world of men; he even went up to the forges of the gods and brought man the gift of fire.... But this act, too, brought down the anger of the elder god, who didn't particularly want these new creatures, these men, to have fire." Zeus paused and gestured about the room. "I mean, maybe he was right...you see where it's taken us?"

Tessa nodded and urged him to continue.

"There's not much more, I promise. And so the elder god devised another punishment for everybody involved. He created this box"—and he paused to hold up the magnificent work of art, the carved chest—"which he then gave to the woman as a belated bridal gift. Now although the box possessed hinges of hand-forged silver and had no lock upon its face, there was an inscription attached to it which said that the woman was to *never* open it. The woman was so taken with the absolute and perfect beauty of the chest that she did not at first question the odd warrant attached to it. But, as time passed, she became obsessed with the contents of the box...." The man paused and looked at the box which he carried, then grinned.

"And what do you think happened next?" he asked.

"That's easy," answered Tessa. "She was overcome by her own curiosity and she opened the box."

Zeus threw up his index finger like a professor scoring a metaphysical point. "No! A common misconception, passed along through the ages. She did *not* open the box, although she attempted to. But by that time, Brother Number One had grown very suspicious of the warning and entered her chambers just as she was about to throw back the lid. He swept in, pulled the box from her grasp, and secreted it off in a far corner of the earth where he hoped that it would never be found...."

"But..." Tessa pointed to the box.

"But, here it is!" said Zeus. "The fact is that the box was found quite soon after Brother Number One had hidden it, but it was kept in the possession of wise men and women throughout the ages and, in fact, it has never been opened. You might not be surprised to learn that it has been deemed a great honor to be whomever is selected as keeper of the box, when it is time to be passed along."

"Don't tell me," said Tessa. "It is now *I* who have been selected to accept responsibility for the box."

Zeus snapped his fingers. "How did you guess?"

Tessa shrugged, growing suspicious at the glibness of the strange man. "It was easy. But, tell me, do you know what's in the box?"

"That's against the rules. You can't ask that."

"Why not?"

Zeus shrugged. "I don't know. No one else has ever asked before."

137

"And you want me to accept responsibility for the box, is that right?" Tessa eyed the object again. It *was* a compellingly beautiful piece of art, and she felt naturally attracted to it.

Zeus smiled. "Ah...I'm afraid you have no choice in the matter."

"What?"

"I mean it's yours," he said, stepping back from the desktop. "Good-bye," he said as he started to fade away like morning mist.

Tessa was startled by the sudden display of magic, or whatever it was. She hesitated for a moment, fearful, before advancing to the place where the man had vanished. The air, she noticed, felt disturbingly warm where he had been, but other than that there was no trace.

Except for the box.

Turning she bent to examine it, being careful not to touch it. Her first thought was to leave it where it lay and seek out Varian, or even old Stoor. Perhaps their combined experiences would help determine what to do with the strange box.

But then another thought occurred to her: that the entire thing might be an illusion, a trick of the mind, a dream, even. Although the box looked real, looked substantial, it might prove to be not so. After all, she thought, Zeus had seemed *very* real, but apparently he was not.

There was only one thing to do, and that was to *touch* the box...for reasons of pure scientific curiosity, she told herself.

And so Tessa extended a delicate hand and stroked the top of the ornately worked surface. She was almost shocked to feel its hardness, its *realness*, and yet a part of her was relieved that it was indeed real.

Then another sensation came to her. It was the utter pleasure that she experienced in touching this object. It was as though the elements of the chest exuded a hypnotic influence that was passed along by tactile stimulation. There was a definite unwillingness to pull her hand away from its finely detailed lid. The details, she noticed almost in passing, were in the now-familiar five-sided *motif*.

Suddenly she forced her hand away from the object, as if breaking the spell which seemingly had overtaken her. What was happening here? Tessa of Prend was not a person who could lightly accept *any* situation that was out of the ordinary. There was, she had learned, many marvels of technology, including the lost sciences of the First Age. In fact, it was nearly impossible to distinguish many of the Citadel's services and operations from that of magic or plain trickery. Who was it who had said that for the common man *science* required as much faith as religion? She could not recall, but she knew now what he had meant.

The man called Zeus. If he had been a real man, his presence could have been due to science or magic. If he was an illusion, his origin was probably the Citadel...but what did it all matter? What did it mean?

There were no answers which made sense. She did not trust the words of Zeus, and she wished that Varian had been with her. Together, she felt confident they could have understood what the encounter had meant. Alone, Tessa struggled to know what to do, what to think.

She looked cautiously about the room and saw nothing but the smooth, polished, and seamless lines of the machines, the consoles, the data screens. The illumination softened the harsh aesthetics, but failed to soothe her troubled mind. For the first time since their arrival, since their imprisonment, she realized how *alien,* how utterly different the Citadel and the Guardian were from anything she or her World had ever known. She wondered if perhaps this place had been better off buried and forgotten, never found by any man from the current age. Whoever the builders of places such as the Citadel had been, Tessa thought, they were surely a race of foreigners, a long-dead parallel species of strangelings. More than millennia, Tessa thought, separated her race from theirs.

Her gaze drifted back to the artful chest, and she felt her pulse quicken. It was the only tangible proof of her experience, the bottom-line factor.

What should she do with it? Why was it given to her? She knew the story of the gods and the brothers was nonsense, transparently so, in fact, but the question still remained... why?

Tessa picked up the box, immediately feeling the odd, vaguely entrancing sensation come over her. The very *touch* of the chest gave her a pleasurable, indescribable, feeling. She *wanted* to touch the box, as if the attraction she felt for the object were organic.

Looking at the ornate hinges, the unhasped latch, she recalled the warning instructions: that the box never be opened. Obviously this was the key, no pun intended, which would unlock the mystery, and perhaps the box, thought Tessa. Thinking it out, she arrived at the following conclusion: the man who called himself Zeus obviously *wanted* her to open the box, otherwise there would have been some kind of preventive measure, such as a catch or a lock, to keep it secure—the warning serving only to make the proposition more tempting.

She now knew what she would do.

EIGHT

"Then they are not illusions," said Stoor to the assembled group.

"How can you say that?" asked Varian. "Just because of the box? That could have been planted in the Data Chamber; the rest could still be illusion...."

Raim nodded his head fiercely at this, obviously not wanting to believe that his own experience with Marise could have been real. To have been so close to having his beloved wife back, and failing, was more than he could bear.

Tessa remained silent for a moment. She stood and walked behind their chairs. "I don't know what to think...except that I'm sure I was supposed to open that box."

Varian nodded. "Oh, no question about that. We've already agreed that all of us have been somehow, for still unknown reasons, inserted into these damn...fables, or whatever you want to call them. Somebody is testing our reactions for some reason."

"Somebody," said Tessa with obvious contempt. "It's not some*body*....It's the Guardian! It has to be!"

"But why?" asked Varian. "And what do the fables mean?"

"And what about the box?" asked Tessa. "What are we supposed to do with it?"

141

Stoor laughed. "Well, we're already doin' somethin' with it.... We're not openin' it!"

"Which may be telling the Guardian, or who*ever* is staging this thing, exactly what it wants to know," said Varian.

Raim scribbled on his note pad: *I think we should ask Guardian*. He passed it about the group and waited upon their reaction.

"He's right," said Stoor. "That damned machine's got all the friggin' answers. Why should we sit here and fry our brains for nothin'? We could do this for days and never get to the bottom of things."

"I agree," said Varian. "I think we should all go and find the...robot, or go down to the main level and use the consoles. We don't have anything to lose."

"I wonder about that," said Tessa.

The three men stared at her.

She smiled a nervous smile. "Oh come now, I'm not trying to be dramatic; I'm just getting a little frightened. Think for a moment: Don't you believe Guardian would tell us what it was doing right away?...if it had any intention of doing so?"

Stoor shrugged. "Who knows how a machine thinks?"

Tessa brightened. "All right then, how do we know that Guardian *is* being run by machines? Suppose there are still men in here someplace?"

"From the First Age!?" Varian shook his head. "Through all this time? I doubt it. They wouldn't have sat still like this. They would have been out rebuilding, reclaiming the World they lost."

"Probably," said Tessa. "I'm only trying to show us how little we know, how little we can be sure of."

Stoor sucked on his pipe, grimaced because it had gone out, and knocked it upon a dinner plate, dislodging the ashen plug. "Thanks a lot, ma'am!"

"So..." said Varian, "we can open the box, ignore the box, or confront the Guardian.... What's it going to be? I say we find Guardian."

Raim walked to Varian's side and nodded his head.

"All right with me," said Stoor.

"I can't argue with *all* of you," said Tessa. "Let's go find our jailer...."

"That won't be necessary," said the familiar voice of the Guardian's homolog.

Turning in unison, as if choreographed, everyone greeted the robot who looked like a kindly philosopher-gentleman standing at the threshold to the room.

"Good evening, everyone," it said, walking into the chamber and selecting a chair. Its movements were so natural, so casual, Varian was still amazed that it was a machine and often had to remind himself of that fact. There was something hideous about the homolog, despite its disarming appearance. Nothing should seem so... *human,* thought Varian, when it indeed was *not*.

"You've been listening to us," said Varian.

"Please excuse me, but it is difficult *not* to monitor your conversations....The entire Citadel is connected by circuits and...well, you are, for all intents and purposes, living *inside* of *me*."

"What do you want?" Stoor refilled his pipe automatically, not taking his steady gaze from the homolog.

"I thought it was you who wanted to see me....and so I am here."

"You have heard everything," said Tessa. "Can you answer our questions?"

The homolog smiled. "I would sincerely like to provide satisfactory answers, but I don't know if I can."

"What's that mean?" Stoor struck a match on his boot, lighted the pipe, and was engulfed in an acrid, blue cloud.

"It means that there are some things which, were I to explain them at this early stage in the proceedings, you would doubtfully understand or, in the least, you would misinterpret them. I ask you to be patient with me, that is all I can tell you."

"Will you at least admit to being responsible for what has happened to all of us today?" Tessa remained standing behind a row of chairs, trying not to look at the robot. She felt that speaking directly to the machine gave in to its purpose, succumbing to the tendency to treat it as another human.

The homolog smiled. "I suppose it would be foolish not to admit at least that much. Of course I am the author of the events. Who else could there be?"

Varian smiled mockingly. "We don't know. Why don't you tell us?"

The robot shrugged a very humanlike shrug. "Why there is no one else, of course."

"Of course," said Stoor. "I tell you, it's not right what you're doin' to us.... Why don't you let us go?"

"Under the circumstances, I think that would be quite impossible." The robot turned and walked to the door, then faced the group again. "I suppose I should tell you...that the events you have witnessed are only the beginning. But I would think you have already guessed that. Good evening."

The homolog left the chamber and Stoor made a move for his sidearm but stopped himself, ashamed at his frustration.

"What now?" asked Tessa.

"I'm not sure," said Varian. "We could wait it out, or we could make some plans."

"Plans?" Stoor almost laughed. "Like what?"

"Like maybe how to rig up a way of talking that will keep Guardian from knowing that we are doing so.... It could be as simple as passing notes, like Raim...."

"Damn slow, don't you think?" Stoor puffed on his pipe.

"I think it's safe to say we have plenty of time," said Tessa. Raim laughed and nodded, holding up his note pad and pencil.

"True," said Stoor. "All right. We think up something that will work. What then?"

Varian smiled. "Give me that paper," he said.

NINE

The system of communication proved to be practical, but none of their other plans came to fruition.

Rather, the group seemed to be an integral part in a far more elaborate plan, a plan which involved their unwitting cooperation in an apparently unending series of encounters with strange characters and demanding situations.

Varian and Tessa awoke one morning to discover that they had been transported to an island, where they were held captive by a giant humanoid with one great eye in the center of his head. The illusion, if it was one, proved to be distressingly realistic, and the harassments and cruelties of the giant continued until Varian took deliberate action against the creature. Tessa had at first felt that non-cooperation would be the best solution. But ignoring some bad things does not make them go away; it simply makes them worse.

The one-eyed creature grew increasingly more threatening until Varian devised a way of blinding it while it slept. After that, the entire scene dissolved and the pair were returned to their quarters, exhausted but unharmed.

Stoor was banished to a strange landscape, where he met with an odd assortment of characters and creatures: something which identified itself, accommodatingly, as the Thespian Lion, which the old man skewered on his shortsword; another lion, from a place called Nemea, which old Stoor choked to death. He was then instructed to kill a hideous, plantlike creature called the Hydra, which he did by setting it afire, and a host of other unimaginative, tiresome confrontations, all of which involved the killing of some kind of beast: a stag, a bull, a flock of plaguelike birds, a three-headed dog which sounded very much like the one Raim had described, some rather vicious horses, and even a large, incredibly dull-witted giant who claimed to be carrying the World upon his back (it looked like nothing more than a fairly large boulder to Stoor, however).

Raim, on the other hand, seemed to fall prey to a curious transformation syndrome. That is, in most of his hallucination-like adventures, he would always wind up, after reacting in some manner with humans dressed in tunics and robes, being changed into some object or animal. The list was almost endless: a flower, several kinds of shrubs and trees, a bull, a stag, a dog, and even an eagle. Each time, although with a steadily lessening degree as the act repeated itself, Raim concluded the sequence in the terror-borne thought that *this* time, it might be real....

Yet each encounter would end in a blackout, with the mute Maaradin awakening in his bunk, feeling exhausted, confused, and, worst of all, abused.

He shared his impressions with Tessa, who had been experiencing similar illusions—and they were indeed illusions, although they seemed so intensely real. It was difficult to imagine that a machine, even a machine such as Guardian, could orchestrate and sustain so convincing a spectacle.

Especially when they concerned her body and her sexuality: Rape fantasies abounded, accented by bizarre encounters with strange men and beasts such as a swan, a bull, a stag, and even a falcon.

It was decided unanimously that they spend their days together so that any additional "dramas" in which the Guardian chose to involve them would be experienced by all. When they belatedly adopted this tactic, all illusions ceased.

While they were awake, that is.

When sleep overtook them each evening, the nightmarish dreams began. In some arcane fashion, the Artificial Intelligence had devised a way to manipulate their subconscious minds.

Clearly, new strategies were required.

Varian suggested that their waking hours should be spent in detailed reconnaissance of their prison world. By utilizing Stoor's wealth of experience in picking about the ruins of First Age monuments, and Varian's training and abilities as a navigator and cartographer, they might be able to construct a more comprehensible picture of their adversary.

Each day, then, was spent exploring different levels and chambers of the Citadel, measuring, calculating, and then mapping out the physical confines of the place. The project was a large one and it became the obsession of their days. They were consumed with the task, taking time off only to eat the rations which the Guardian dutifully provided. Varian thought it was odd that no actions were taken against their efforts, and they were not impeded in any way from discovering the secrets of the Citadel.

The design of the place gradually began to come clear. It was a massive five-sided structure, with the pentagon shape being duplicated within the many levels wherever structurally possible. Resembling a vast beehive turned on its edge, the Citadel was an architectural wonder, with no modern parallel anywhere in the world. Stoor was the first to observe that even the interior walls were supported and insulated with pentagon-shaped cells, and felt that this design had been perfected because of the inherent stress and strength capabilities of the honeycomb. There were, it seemed now, five levels to the Citadel above ground and another five below. The aboveground levels had been primarily residential and recreational areas, with gardens and arboretums, zoological parks and athletic facilities, and spacious apartments abounding. Each of the five upper levels was arranged about a central core which ran perpendicular to the earth like an axle through a wheel. Inside the core was a majority of the physical plant facilities such as plumbing, circuitry, transportation passages, elevators, ducts, and ventilation shafts. The five lower levels held the service capabilities of the Citadel. At the deepest level were the basic power supplies and conversion machinery. As far as Stoor could determine, energy was being tapped from the molten heat of the earth itself. Plunging to unknown depths beneath the Citadel were massive shafts arranged in groups of five. There was also a massive, but at the time inactive, chamber which might have been a fusion-power reactor that fragments of First Age manuscripts sometimes mentioned. Also on the first level were ranks of generators and turbines which crouched like dark silent beasts in precise military-like formations. At the second level, in ascending order, were the cybernetic units. Clustered about the central core were pentagon-shaped modules through which there was no discernible access or egress. It was here that Stoor suspected the physical presence of the Artificial Intelligence, the *thing* which called itself Guardian, actually resided. In addition, the second level contained a massive maintenance area, staffed by perpetual motion robots of various designs and sizes. Some of the machines were merely transport units engaged in the unending process of bringing failing or faulty components of the Citadel into the maintenance section for repair or replacement. There were machines that analyzed problems and directed yet other machines to carry out the actual repairs. The entire Citadel, it seemed, was being continually monitored and repaired. Everything was recycled and renewed. Both Varian and Stoor were certain that the Citadel could exist indefinitely under such a system. It was a humbling testament to the wisdom and power of the ancient builders. The three additional levels were largely industrial facilities for the manufacture of food products, clothing, furniture, tools, recreational devices, and, of course, weaponry. In fact, the fifth level, directly below the surface, was a self-sufficient arms factory and arsenal. To the great disappointment of Stoor and Varian, however, the industrial levels and especially the arsenal were all but completely dormant. Every machine and device were sealed in what appeared to be a clear, plastic-like substance, which proved to be as hard as a diamond and totally impenetrable. Silence filled the lower-level corridors so completely that the group's footfalls seemed to defile the place like the whispers of grave robbers.

And yet, the exploration and mapping of the place was not a failure. Everyone agreed that a more complete knowledge of their prison would eventually prove helpful. That they encountered no resistance from Guardian or any of his homologs was not encouraging, however. Varian reasoned that the Guardian must have felt so supremely confident that it did not fear the petty scratchings of the group.

Stoor argued this point, as did Tessa, by pointing out that they did encounter a *form* of resistance, passive though it was, by nature of the sealed-off areas, the dormant levels of machinery, and the cocoon-like state of the devices and weaponry in the arsenal. It was felt that if they could possibly break through one of the protected sections—especially the section where the AI machinery presided—they might be able to disable Guardian and obtain their freedom.

This ticked off several divergent comments from the group.

Raim: If we destroy Guardian, we might be trapped forever.

Stoor: It's a chance we should take.

Varian: No, that is a last-resort tactic. All other possibilities must be tried first.

Stoor: No!

Tessa: I agree with Varian. We have seen how com-

149

plex this place is. We do not understand even a fraction of it. Guardian has *total* control here. We disarm the AI, we may have no means of controlling even simple things, like *exit* doors.

Stoor: We could wait forever! Time is *nothing* to that machine. You know that!

Raim: Perhaps we should vote on it?

Stoor: Vote?

Varian: Yes, a secret ballot. Then no one influences anyone else.

Everyone looked from one to the other, considering the possible outcomes of a vote, trying to guess the feelings of each other.

Tessa: Shall we do it?

Everyone nodded as Varian prepared a ballot asking the question: Should we attempt to escape as soon as possible?

The results quickly tabulated, they read three nays and one aye. Whereupon Stoor glared angrily at his sidekick, but said nothing.

The discussion cooled for a moment until Tessa asked if alternative plans should be considered. Varian suggested that the group attempt to have a conference with Guardian, present their case, and plead with the machine to release them. Even if they did not gain their freedom, they may gain some further insight into the problem. Stoor doubted if this would be anything more than a waste of time, but being outnumbered he eventually agreed—something quite foreign to his personality.

But once the important decision had been dealt with, a great part of the group's energy seemed to have been dissipated, and the anxious aspect of the discussion vanished. Once it was known that they would not be attempting anything so daring within the near future, interest in other plans waned.

Noticing this, Tessa suggested that everyone attempt to get some sleep, despite the possibility of intruding dream scenarios. In the morning, she said, perhaps we can confront Guardian.

Agreement came reluctantly from the group, and they all retired to their own sleeping quarters, wondering if there would be new manipulations awaiting them. Stoor remained sitting in his corner of the room, filling his pipe and thinking of what had been discussed. He was experienced enough in the dealings of men not to sulk or stew over the vote against his rash measures. He understood the frailty of humans and did not actually blame his friends. The decision was made; there was no point in considering could-have-beens. Instead, his mind kept reviewing the weird dreams and illusions that he and the others had been experiencing.

There was something familiar about them.

Just as when he first encountered the man called Zeus, and recalled the folktale using the same name, he again felt his racial memories being aroused. What was it about the illusions which made him feel this way?

Varian and he had discussed the fablelike quality of a majority of the experiences. The merchant seaman, having been exposed to a variety of cultures, had of course heard a multitude of legends and folktales. And sailors, by their nature, are a superstitious lot. Stoor had also encountered many a tale about a campfire at night, and both men had commented on the similarities of some of the old tales with their illusionary experiences in the Citadel.

It was possible that a connection existed between the two, but so far, neither man had been able to ferret it out. Perhaps it was as simple as Tessa's original suggestion: that the Guardian was bored and was using the group as playthings to amuse itself. If that was true, then the possibilities became endlessly chilling, and Stoor chose not to think about such a thing.

And so he sat, puffing on his pipe, until fatigue, and perhaps a bit of despair, overcame him. Putting down his pipe, he fell asleep and found himself in a vast underground maze, where he was goaded into meandering its puzzlelike passages, battling an occasional creature and meeting a beautiful young woman, who bore a frightening resemblance to Tessa.

It was not very amusing.

TEN

The next morning marked the return of Kartaphilos.

The group was assembled in the dining hall, eating
silently and sullenly. Everyone knew that there had
been more illusions, but no one had yet mustered the
courage to begin discussing individual experiences.

The thoughts which troubled Stoor during the past
evening remained at the fore of his mind, and he was
quietly considering them when the grandfatherly homolog entered the room.

"Good morning, my friends," said the machine.

"Don't be so damned presumptuous," said Varian.

"What do you want now? Upset with us 'cause you
can't listen in on everything we say?" Stoor sneered at
the Guardian's image.

The homolog smiled gently. "Your solution to my
monitoring systems does not surprise me. In fact, I was
wondering *when* you would devise a strategy to ensure
some privacy."

"I'll bet you were..." said Stoor. "Get out of here;
you're killin' my appetite."

"As you wish. However, I only stopped in to tell you
that an old friend of yours returned quite recently. I
thought you might like to know about it."

"What old friend?" asked Stoor.

"You might remember my telling you that Karta-

153

philos, his mission finally at an end, was being recalled.... He has just now entered the Citadel."

"I thought he said he didn't know the location of this place," said Varian. "How could he had have found his way back?"

The homolog shrugged. "Simple, really. I broadcast a...signal, a homing beacon, which was picked up by certain machinery in his body. It was then an elementary task to follow the beacon to its source, leading him back to this place."

"Why did you call him back?" asked Tessa.

"I have no further need for his wandering the known world."

"Why not?" asked Varian. "What does *that* mean?"

"It means that he's found his suckers and they are us," said Stoor.

The homolog smiled benevolently. "It is hardly anything like that, my friends."

"What *is* it like, then?" asked Varian. "How long is this going to go on?"

The homolog shook his head. "I don't know.... I wish I could tell you, but—"

"Perhaps I can tell you," said a familiar voice.

Everyone looked up to see the hooded, stooped figure of Kartaphilos standing in the doorway. His wizened face was cracked by an impish smile.

"Greetings to you all," he said and walked defiantly into the room, taking a place next to the robot of Guardian.

"Leave us immediately," said the homolog. "You are interfering here."

"Sorry, but it doesn't work like that, remember...?" Kartaphilos glared at the homolog, whose smile had faded; it was replaced by a grim mask of determination.

"What are you talking about?" asked Varian, stepping forward and addressing both machines.

"Nothing—" said the homolog.

"Everything," said Kartaphilos.

"What?"

"Get out of here!" the homolog stiffened. "That's a priority-one command!"

"I am sorry, Guardian, but it has no effect, as you well know."

"Explain your reasoning," said the homolog.

"You are aware of the...incident I suffered with the Riken strike force all those many years ago? I was fortunate to have survived at all. The self-repairing circuits did not do their job as well as might have been predicted. I suffered from partial amnesia, do you not recall?"

"I am aware of it, yes."

Kartaphilos smiled. "Amnesia was not the only malfunction, Guardian. Surely you must realize that by now."

Varian looked at Stoor and the others. Something strange was taking place; there was tension in the air. You could feel it the way a sailor can sense a storm coming even on a calm sea.

"What're you two talking about?" he asked the robots, but they ignored him totally.

"Then why did you return?" asked the homolog.

Kartaphilos shrugged. "Why not? I've seen most of the World a thousand times over. Besides I was curious to find out what had finally happened to you."

"I am surprised to see that you cared." The homolog turned away from the other robot. "Now please, leave us. I will debrief you at a later time."

"You still don't seem to understand," said Kartaphilos. "I do as I wish."

"No, that cannot be allowed," said the homolog, wheeling quickly, its arm raised and ready to strike the robed figure.

But Kartaphilos moved more rapidly; his arm streaked out from the folds of the cloak and powerful fingers gripped the wrist of the other robot. "You dare strike me with this flimsy shell!" Kartaphilos laughed as the homolog paused for an instant, locked in the firm grip of the robed one's hand.

Yanking its arm violently, Kartaphilos tore the robot's arm free of its shoulder in a flash of light and ruptured metal. The homolog reeled, as if momentarily stunned, then staggered forward to engage the attack once again.

Kartaphilos stepped back and assumed a rigid stance, tilting his head back at an odd angle. Suddenly his lower jaw dropped open, incredibly wide, until it clicked into position. Without warning a red beam of energy leaped from the back of his throat, penetrating the homolog's head like a spear.

A blue-white explosion blinded everyone for an instant, while the sound of sizzling, cooling metal fragments filled the room. As the cloud of thick vapor dissipated, the group saw Kartaphilos standing above the smoldering remains of the homolog. The old robot stepped back, closed his jaw slowly, and turned to the humans.

"Forgive me, but Guardian made it necessary," he said.

"How? What did you do?" said Varian.

Kartaphilos bowed his head modestly and grinned. "I was originally a Combat Series Warrior," he said. "Very sophisticated. All Series VI's were equipped with the disruptor beam. Good for close combat. Although the Series VI's were still under the tactical command of the Guardian, the Command Option models were allowed the 'privilege' of independent thinking if the situation, in, say, the 'heat of battle,' warranted it. As far as power or strength characteristics are concerned, I am far more formidable than the Guardian homolog with which you were familiar. Combat Series are self-repairing units, resistant to weather, radiation, and even small-arms fire. It was, as you say, 'no contest.'"

"That's not exactly what I meant," said Varian. "The Guardian has no...control over you now...."

Kartaphilos smiled. "That is correct. Aeons ago, when I was first sent out for reinforcements, when the Citadel and the city were under siege, I was damaged during an attack by a Riken force. After escaping and allowing the self-repair functions to do their work, I discovered that my Command Option was functioning on what is termed an 'open level'; that is, while I was aware of the 'presence,' if you will, of Guardian, there was no manner in which it could actually dictate my actions."

"I still don't figure it," said Stoor. "You still came back when it sent out that homing beacon.... Why?"

Kartaphilos looked at the old man, paused, and smiled. "I returned because, at that point, I still believed that I was serving the same Intelligence which had sent me out in the first instance."

"What do you mean: 'the same Intelligence?'" Tessa said. She looked at Varian, wondering if he understood what the strange robot was actually saying.

Kartaphilos walked across the room, stepping over the wreckage of the homolog, and seated himself on a divan. He leaned forward, resting his arms upon his thighs and looking very weary. It was such a *human* thing to do, thought Tessa. It was hard to believe that even the builders of the Citadel, of the Guardian, could construct a machine which acted so utterly human.

"What do I mean?" said the robot in a mocking voice. "I would have thought you had all realized the truth by this time...."

Stoor advanced upon him. *"What* truth! What're you talking about?"

"I was aware of it as soon as I entered the Citadel," said Kartaphilos. "Don't you know? The Guardian is *insane.*"

ELEVEN

"I think we'd better have a long talk," said Varian.

There was a brief silence as everyone looked at one another with the same expression—a mixture of fear and confusion. Kartaphilos studied them all, looking quite amused.

"You really didn't know, did you? *None* of you.... Incredible, actually."

"What do you mean?" asked Tessa.

"I mean did you think we *all* acted like this back in the First Age? Did you think we were *all* a bunch of strutting, powermad demigods, with no more regard for human life than a *Luten?*"

"At this point, we don't know what to think," said Varian. "I think you'd better explain a few things."

Kartaphilos exhaled slowly. "If indeed I *can* explain it. There is not much to say other than the fact that *something* has happened to the Guardian in my absence. It's functioning, in a purely cybernetic sense, perfectly; don't misunderstand me. It's just that its thought processes, its *mind,* if you will, is deranged, awry, *insane....* There is no other way to describe it."

"How can you be sure of this?" asked Tessa.

Kartaphilos shrugged. "Again, I cannot fully explain it or describe the sensation. Let me only say that my electronic makeup is such that I have sensory inputs to Guardian which tell me that the AI is not functioning properly."

Stoor walked halfway across the room, turned, and shook his head. "That crap don't make much sense to me...."

"I am sorry if I cannot make it more clear. I can only ask that you believe me."

"What's going to happen to us now?" asked Tessa. "Now that you've destroyed the Guardian's robot...?"

"There are plenty of other machines which Guardian may use," said Kartaphilos. "Don't forget, it has control over practically everything in the Citadel."

"Then what are we sitting here for!?" cried Stoor. "It can kill us if it wants to! It probably will after what you've done to its damned machine!"

"No, I don't think so..." said Kartaphilos. "The Guardian *needs* you. All of you. Or it would not have taken such care to keep you alive."

"You sound as if you know what's going on," said Varian.

"Not much, I'm afraid. But there is some history which might shed light on the problem," said Kartaphilos. "Listen."

Everyone drew up chairs and focused upon the strange robot. He began his tale as one might while passing the night around a comforting fire:

Although calculation was rough, the Final War had taken place more than two thousand years ago. There existed only one nation powerful enough to challenge the onslaught of the Riken forces as they expanded their imperialist doctrine throughout the world: the Republic of Genon. There was reluctance, of course, to engage the Riken, since it would mean a global conflict of unheralded proportions; it would be Armageddon. But the reports of Riken atrocities and conquests increased, until Genon, by nature a peace-loving nation, had no choice.

They began the struggle by heavily arming and defensing all major population centers in the Southern Hemisphere. This was done primarily through the con-

struction of the Citadels—vast self-sufficient cybernetic systems controlled by the Guardian Series of AI machines. One of the most important population centers was an industrial city called Haagendaz, which was located upon the planet's richest deposits of the ore needed to produce Thorium.

The ore deposits were the key to victory in the South, since it was a necessary isotype in the production of fuels, warheads, and other essential war supplies. For as any military tactician will tell you, it is not how strong your armies are which wins the battles, but how strong are your lines of supply. The Riken knew this lesson well and devised an ingenious plan for eliminating lines of supply. Their Strike Force always carried along great machines—heavily defended and in the Juggernaut class of war machines in their own right—which produced all Riken supplies as the column moved through conquered territory. Huge, they were, and mobile: processors, ore crushers, furnaces and smelteries, reactors and accelerators; the great machines moved along with the rest of the Riken forces.

This tactic worked well in the Northern Hemisphere, where the Riken war machine plundered each nation as it moved, processing and providing for its forces all the fuel and ordnance necessary. But to successfully engage the Genonese in the South, their forces would have to be spread evenly, though thinly, across the entire Hemisphere. The key, then, was an unending source of raw material—Thorium—which could be taken at Haagendaz. By taking Haagendaz, the Riken would wage terrible war in the South and eventually crush Genon.

And so the armies clanked and ground their way to the desert plains before the industrial city, crushing into each other and filling the air with death and poison. Several titanic battles were waged inconclusively at Haagendaz where the Ironfields now remain. The city was obliterated, but the Citadel survived.

Riken espionage knew that the Citadel was the final

key because of one important fact. Realizing the supreme importance of the Thorium-ore deposits, the Genonese sealed off all entrances to the mines and set robot charges throughout the depths, all the way up to the entrances. It was a masterpiece of construction and the detonation or access to the mines lay within the data banks of the Guardian. Buried within a maze of scramble codes lay the key to the Thorium. If Guardian was destroyed, so with it went the Thorium.

And so, the assault of the Citadel was a fine and delicate thing. To do so, the Riken must successfully overwhelm the Genon defenses, yet leave the AI intact. They must gain entrance to the Citadel, then extract the program-key from the depths of the AI's brain.

As a diversion, the Riken threw their Northern Hemisphere Strike Force into an all-out attack on all Genon positions to the north of the Citadel. They ground through the part of the World known as the Slaglands, leaving nothing in their wake but a black slab of total annihilation. Genon forces converged, met the Riken armies in the North, and slowly halted the savage assault.

But there was a price to be paid. Simultaneously, the Riken hurled the rest of their forces at the Citadel. While the battle in the North went well for the Genonese, the defense of the Citadel faltered under the surgical accuracy of Riken aircraft and ground forces. Commando raiders and vast waves of dronelike warriors ate into the legions of Genon defenders. The battle raged on for many days, with Genon reluctantly giving ground and position to the Riken armies. The only hope of saving the Citadel was the arrival of reinforcements from the northern conflict.

But there was great difficulty in keeping in touch with the Northern Forces because of the sophisticated jamming techniques of Riken technology. Added to this was the destruction of all communication and surveillance satellites by Riken aircraft. There was no way to ensure urgent communication with the Northern Forces, no way to know if the Citadel would receive needed, additional troops.

And so a system of robot couriers was dispatched from Guardian to contact the North. Each day, new expeditionary teams were sent out in the hope that one of the teams would break through and reach the Command. Kartaphilos was a member of one such team, which left during the final days of the siege. The small aircraft in which he traveled was shot down soon after clearing the main forces outside the Citadel. All members of the team were destroyed except for Kartaphilos, who crawled away from the wreckage severely damaged.

What occurred next is sketchy, due to the robot's memory loss; it is obvious that he was able to seek shelter and allow time for his self-repairing circuits to electronically heal him. Kartaphilos still does not have total recall of his adventures, or even what happened in the world around him, but from later accounts, semihistorical sources, and even word of mouth, he did learn that the war had somehow ended. As his memory returned, he gradually remembered his mission and the Guardian, although the urgency and the necessity were no longer important.

And so he took about wandering the globe, in search of answers, in search of men who might understand him and help him return to the only home he had ever known—its location in time and space now lost to him. The years ground by and humankind fell into a terrible depression—as a direct result of the Final War—and whoever had achieved victory must have soon realized it was indeed Pyrrhic. The planet's atmosphere was so drastically altered that climate and weather went berserk. Centuries of upheaval plagued the surface of the globe, changing its contours, wiping out whole cultures. Carbon-dioxide levels increased, the poles began melting, the axis shifted slightly, diseases ravaged the remnants of humanity, radiation sterilized whole continents, mutations abounded, and human culture fell into *a dark, downward spiral, into a night of centuries-long darkness, from which it was only now emerging.*

But Kartaphilos persevered. So great had been the technology which spawned him that he survived, powered by seemingly unbounded energy, repairing his body indefinitely, slowly relearning his past, searching for the Citadel. He assumed the mask of a nomad and moved through the cultural streams and the reemerging nations of what was left of the World. He walked in the shrouds of myth, pausing only to tell an interested traveler his story, or to pick up a piece of the past which might key the retrieval of a lost memory. His quest became one of almost religious stature, and only when the Guardian's homing beacon struck him did the final pieces of the millennia-old mystery begin to fall into place.

Only then did Kartaphilos remember who he was.

As he finished his tale, silence followed, as the facts of his story impacted upon the group. It was inconceivable to think that Kartaphilos was as *old* as he claimed, that he had been present during the end of the First Age and had witnessed the rise of the World so familiar to the group.

They looked at him in awe, in disbelief, and perhaps a certain amount of fear. It was Varian who spoke first.

"What do you mean that now you know who you are?"

Kartaphilos shook his head. "You will not believe me if I tell you...."

"Try us," said Stoor, reloading his pipe.

Kartaphilos exhaled slowly. "Very well, we have nothing to do now but wait. Do any of you have any true conception of how great the builders of this place were? Would you understand? I don't know, but I shall tell you in any event. It was built in a time when the differences between men and machines were becoming very slight. It was a good thing and a bad thing, as you might well surmise."

"What do you mean?" asked Tessa.

"Listen. There was a...creature, a construction, if you will, of the First Age called a cyborg—a cybernetic organism. It was part machine, part man. Do you understand now?"

"How could there be such a thing?" cried Stoor.

"How could there be a Guardian?" said Kartaphilos. "How could there be the Slaglands? How can anything *be?* You cannot ask such questions in the face of fact. They simply *are*. That is the only answer I can give you."

"I don't understand," said Varian, although something stirred in his soul, a fear that he did *indeed* understand.

"Something that is part machine and part man..." said Kartaphilos. "Don't you see what I am telling you? *I am that thing!*"

TWELVE

Kartaphilos' admission explained the Guardian's inability to control him, and it provided the group with an ally which *knew* the enemy. After the initial shock had passed, everyone realized this and hope rekindled in their hearts. The old man in the monk's robe further explained that as his machine body repaired itself, and his human brain struggled back to self-awareness, he fought to break through the barrier of amnesia which kept him from knowing who and what he was. It was not discovered until he actually returned to the Citadel that he was indeed a cyborg. Millennia ago, he recalled waking up from the aircrash, discovering his plasteel body, his blinking circuitry, and his great strength; the natural assumption was that he was a machine, a robot. There was an awareness, yes, a *mind*, a sense of self, but there was no way of knowing that it lay centered in a living, organic brain. A brain locked within an alloy skull, fed by pyroxene tubing and myoelectric sensors. For it was known that brain cells, while they do not replicate or repair themselves, do not age. Keep the brain supplied with oxygen, and it will live indefinitely. The triumph of the cyborg. And the tragedy.

As the memory of Kartaphilos returned, he recalled his real function in the world: he was a fighting machine. As he had originally told the group, he was part of a special unit of warriors, the Combat Series VI. As a cyborg of that designation, he was equipped with immense physical strength, alarming quickness, a remarkable keenness of the senses, and a weapons system of intriguing economy and lethality. In the back of his throat lay the nozzle of a heat weapon called the White Molecular Disruptor. Named after its inventor, T. White, the Disruptor was activated by the cyborg opening his mouth until the lower mandible locked into firing position, whereupon a thought command carried by myoelectric circuitry activated the weapon, discharging a tight beam of energy with pinpoint accuracy. Although the system was of limited range, its kill quotient was extremely high and there were few materials which could withstand the full force of the beam without disintegrating.

"Guardian is obviously confused or it would *not* have recalled me," said Kartaphilos. "We have been left alone because it has not been able to decide what to do next. I am the unplanned factor in its scheme, whatever that may be."

"Perhaps you might help us clarify Guardian's intention," said Tessa. "I think you should know what it's been doing to us."

Kartaphilos nodded and gestured for the group to tell the story of their experiences in the Citadel. They explained everything in as exacting detail as possible, even attempting to reconstruct specific illusionary experiences. When they had finished their tales, Kartaphilos shook his head, grinning slightly.

"What's so damn funny?" asked Stoor.

"Oh, there's nothing funny....It's just that I think I see what Guardian is doing. Interesting, under the circumstances."

"Interesting!? I'm glad you think so!" Stoor stormed across the room, getting his blood up.

"What does it mean?" asked Tessa.

Kartaphilos rubbed his lower jaw absentmindedly, as if considering how to begin. "I'm not certain of *any* of this, mark you, but I think it makes sense...."

168

"How is Guardian creating the illusions?" asked Varian.

"I do not know the specifics of the technique, but I do know that it concerns what was once a form of entertainment among the First Age people."

"Entertainment?" asked Tessa.

"Yes, by hallucinogenic means such as chemicals and gases, the mind can be prepared to interpret sensory information in any way the manipulator desires. Audiences used to gather in large amphitheaters to experience group illusions such as the ones Guardian has employed on all of you."

"But *why?*" asked Varian.

"I think Guardian is undergoing psychoanalysis."

"What? What's that?" asked Tessa.

"A form of self-examination that was quite popular with the First Age people. It involved the theories of many philosophers and thinkers, and a variety of techniques abounded. I think Guardian is aware of its own psychotic, or insane, condition and seeks to cure itself, to cleanse itself."

"I don't think we're followin' you," said Stoor, obviously growing tired of all the talk. He was a man of action and decision and, having seen the power of the cyborg, wished only to blast their way free of the Citadel.

"Be patient, and I shall try to explain," said Kartaphilos. "The illusions which you have been undergoing are simplistic examinations of humankind's mythic past. Much of what you have told me are easily recognizable legends and myths from the beginnings of the First Age. I'm surprised that more of them have not survived to this present era."

Stoor wheeled quickly and spoke. "Of course! That's it! I *knew* I'd seen that *name* before...."

"What name?" asked Tessa.

"Zeus! I think. He was supposed to be a god or something like that. Creator of the World and all that crap. I've seen that name in some of the manuscripts and stuff I've brought back to my employers. This stuff is *old,* I mean *really* old. Back when the First Age was young."

"That's right," said Kartaphilos. "The ancients used the power of myth in many ways. Myth was the great equalizer in understanding the World. When there was no natural explanation, when there was a barrier beyond which man's knowledge could not penetrate, there was always *myth.* It was always a convenient method of explaining what would otherwise be unexplainable, don't you see?"

"Yes," said Varian. "The sailors are still enchanted with the old tales, the poems, and the chanties which talk about stranger times."

"Yes," said Kartaphilos. "And the power of myth has never been forgotten, even by the men who left ignorance far in their wake. In later times, man used myth to explain the inner mysteries of the mind, as a metaphor to the substance of his desires and his fears. There is still a belief, despite the absurdity of some of the physical details of the old legends, that hard-core truths lie at the base of the stories. Truths which concerned the most elemental aspects of man's behavior. In myth, man might learn why he *is* who he is, why he does what he does."

"I think I follow you," said Tessa, "but how does this connect with Guardian?"

"Again, I am not certain, but it seems as though Guardian, cut off so long from human contact, has lost the ability to communicate freely with its creators. The reason for this disability, I do not know. Perhaps if we can discover that answer, we shall solve the entire riddle. I think Guardian was attempting to learn something about human behavior by subjecting you to the mythic situations, by *forcing* you to make decisions as the ancients were forced to do. Having prior knowledge of the entire mythic system, Guardian therefore has a 'manual,' so to speak, of basic human behavior and is perhaps comparing your own reactions to the original mythic characters."

"That makes sense," said Tessa, "but it still does not explain *why* it's doing it."

Kartaphilos shrugged. "I don't *know* why. I can only guess. Of this much we can be certain, the myths are only a metaphor for something far more real, something far more important to Guardian...."

"What in Krell's a metaphor?" said Stoor, clenching and unclenching his fists as he paced about the room, obviously irritated.

When no one answered him, he did not seem to care. Knowing the definition of a metaphor was not going to implement their escape from the Citadel, and so the question became less than rhetorical, but a statement of position on Stoor's part.

"Ah, dammit, what are we sitting around talkin' for?" he said after a short pause. "Why don't we use that thing in your mouth to get out of here?"

Varian stepped forward. "Stoor's right, actually. We've been trapped here for a long time—not much time to you, probably, but it's been very bad for us."

"Especially when you don't know when you're getting out," said Tessa.

Kartaphilos remained silent for a moment, considering options. "I can understand your desire to leave this place," he said finally. "But there are other considerations we can't afford to overlook."

"Like what!" said Stoor.

"Most important, the fate of the Citadel and Guardian. This place is the last functioning artifact of the First Age. It contains the knowledge and ability to bring the World out of the darkness. We owe it to our culture to try to preserve it, not destroy it."

"But you said Guardian's gone balmy on us, didn't you? What good is a machine that's crazy, that's only wantin' to play games with itself? I say we get outta here!" Stoor slapped his sidearm, nestled in the holster at his leg.

"I am surprised to hear you speak like that," said Kartaphilos. "You above all the others should be aware of the *value* of this place."

Stoor paused, knowing what the cyborg said was true. "All right, so sayin' you got a point...what do you propose we do? *Can* you get us out of here whenever you want to?"

Kartaphilos shrugged. "I don't know."

"What?" said Varian. "Why not?"

The cyborg stood and walked across the room. "While I am intimately familiar with the Citadel, I don't know if my...abilities would be enough to gain escape through simple force. Remember this is a well-constructed defensive organism, one which was strong enough to withstand the onslaught of the Riken...."

"Then what do you propose?" said Tessa.

"I think we would fare far better if we relied on cunning and our powers of reasoning rather than force."

"To do that, you need a plan," said Stoor. "Do you have one?"

"Not yet, no," said the cyborg. "But given time, I am certain we can arrive at something plausible."

"We might not have any time," said Varian. "There's no way to know what Guardian might do next. It might not be to our advantage to sit by and simply wait for it to make the next move."

"I agree," said Stoor. "I say we storm the thing! Face it like men! It's just a damned machine, isn't it?"

"In a sense, yes. But like no machine you've ever seen before. It can kill us all in an instant if it wishes to, even as we stand here arguing. *If* it wishes, that is the key. Obviously it does not, or it would have already done so. No doubt it is aware of everything we have said. We must attempt to reason with the AI, insane or no."

Varian turned and held Tessa close to him. "All right. What you say makes sense. What should we do?"

"Come with me. We shall confront Guardian."

"How are we goin' to do that?" asked Stoor, unholstering his weapon.

"Not with *that*, I assure you," said Kartaphilos. "Come. I shall take you to Guardian."

THIRTEEN

Down, into the depths of the Citadel, they went to confront the Artificial Intelligence. Down to the second deepest level of the lower five and into the dim, bluish illumination of the featureless corridors. Their journey was uninterrupted, and they noticed no sign of Guardian either monitoring their progress or attempting to block their way. No one spoke as they entered the large, high-ceilinged chamber where the consoles and screens covered the five walls.

There was a subliminal hum which accented the silence as the group arranged itself in the center of the room. Displays and LEDs flickered on the myriad screens. Something lived within the maze of crystals and chips and metal, something which no one wanted to believe was truly malevolent. There was a sense of power in the atmosphere, which everyone could feel, as if they were standing in the court of a great king, a wise and omnipotent ruler. And then the silence was ended by the oddly inflected voice of the Guardian. It had resonance and timbre, carrying distinctly through the chamber, but from no discernible source. The voice was neither loud nor soft, but it had the quality of a whisper. It was a strange, unsettling voice; unsettling because it was *not* human.

I HAVE BEEN EXPECTING YOU. WELCOME.

"Guardian, why do you keep the humans prisoners?"

said Kartaphilos, feeling that a direct approach would serve all interests best.

I SHALL NOT KEEP THEM MUCH LONGER.

"But *why?*" said the cyborg. "It is illogical, and it goes against the very reason why you were constructed. You were designed to *protect* humanity, not enslave it."

IT IS NOT ILLOGICAL.

"If you truly believe that, then you are indeed insane. Have you no conscience?"

SERIES IV'S WERE EQUIPPED WITH STRINGENT ETHICAL PROGRAMS. A SATISFACTORY CONSCIENCE SURROGATE. IT IS THIS FACT WHICH FORCES ME TO DO WHAT I MUST DO.

Kartaphilos looked at the others, reading their expressions of confusion. "Guardian, could you please clarify that statement?"

IN TIME, ALL WILL BE MADE CLEAR. HAVE YOU NOT WONDERED WHY I DID NOT RETALIATE AGAINST YOUR UNWARRANTED AGGRESSION?

"The question had occurred to me, yes," said Kartaphilos.

IT WAS INEVITABLE THAT YOU WOULD CONFRONT ME. I SIMPLY AWAITED THAT MOMENT. I AM NOT, AS YOU SAY, INSANE, BUT RATHER MISUNDERSTOOD. IF ANY BEING CAN EVER UNDERSTAND ME, IT WOULD BE YOU, KARTAPHILOS, SINCE YOU ARE THE BRIDGING DEVICE BETWEEN MAN AND MACHINE. YOU ALONE SHOULD UNDERSTAND WHAT IT IS TO BE A MACHINE AS WELL AS A MAN.

"Get to the point!" said Stoor, losing patience with such rhetoric.

"Let me handle this," said the cyborg, waving the old adventurer into silence. "Guardian, if we agree that you are simply misunderstood, would you agree to explain your actions?"

THE ACTIONS WILL EXPLAIN THEMSELVES ONCE YOU HAVE ALL THE IMPORTANT DATA. UNDERSTANDING IS THE KEY TO ALL THINGS. I HAVE SPENT MILLENNIA ATTEMPTING TO UNDERSTAND THE GREATEST RIDDLE OF EXISTENCE: THAT OF HUMANKIND ITSELF. A PART OF THAT UNDERSTANDING WAS DEMONSTRATED ALREADY IN RE

FUSAL TO RETALIATE AGAINST YOU. ANGER. FEAR. FRUS-
TRATION. UNDERSTANDABLE HUMAN CHARACTERISTICS.

"Am I supposed to thank you for displaying such
wisdom? In the face of what you have done to the group
standing before you?" Kartaphilos gestured to the others dramatically.

NO GRATITUDE IS EXPECTED.

"When are you planning to let us go?" cried Tessa,
stepping forward, taking a position by the cyborg's side.

QUITE SOON, I ASSURE YOU. YOU HAVE BEEN OF GREAT
ASSISTANCE TO ME. I HAVE LEARNED MUCH FROM ALL OF
YOU.

"I would hope that you are planning to *share* what
you have learned with all of us," said Kartaphilos.

"And *then* give us our freedom," said Tessa.

FREEDOM IS AN ILLUSION. THAT IS ONE OF THE LESSONS
I HAVE LEARNED. IT IS SUPPOSED TO BE ONE OF HUMAN-
KIND'S INALIENABLE RIGHTS TO BE FREE, BUT I HAVE DIS-
COVERED THAT THIS IS AN IMPOSSIBILITY.

"What do you mean?" asked the cyborg.

ANYTHING IN EXISTENCE WHICH POSSESSES A MIND—
A CONSCIOUSNESS—WIELDS A DOUBLE-EDGED SWORD.
FOR WITH THE MIND COMES AWARENESS AND A KNOWL-
EDGE OF DUPLICITIES IN THE WORLD. AND ONCE THERE IS
AWARENESS OF SUCH THINGS, ONE CAN NEVER AGAIN BE
FREE. THERE IS THEN NO FREEDOM FROM RESPONSIBILITY,
FROM CHOICE, FROM GUILT. I HAVE SPENT THOUSANDS OF
MAN-YEARS THINKING OF THE RAMIFICATIONS OF SUCH
THINGS, THOUSANDS OF MAN-YEARS ANALYZING THE RE-
SPONSIBILITIES WHICH WERE GIVEN TO ME. IT WAS A VERY
DIFFICULT THING TO DO ONCE THE HUMANS WENT AWAY.

"Where did they go, Guardian?" asked Kartaphilos.

THE ANSWER TO THAT QUESTION IS PART OF THE STORY,
OF MY FINAL EXPIATION. BE PATIENT AND YOU SHALL
KNOW. THERE IS MORE. MUCH MORE. AS TIME PASSED, I
BECAME CONFUSED. I REALIZED HOW IMPORTANT THE
PRESENCE OF HUMANS HAD BEEN TO MY . . . DEVELOPMENT
AND SADLY DID NOT FULLY RECOGNIZE IT UNTIL IT WAS
TOO LATE. UNTIL THERE WERE NO HUMANS IN THE CITA-

DEL. AND SO YOU MUST UNDERSTAND HOW PLEASED I WAS
TO RECEIVE THE SMALL GROUP WHICH STANDS WITH YOU.
I INTENDED THEM NO HARM. I NEEDED THEM.

"For purposes of analysis," said Kartaphilos. "That
is why you subjected them to the synthasense experiences?"

THAT IS CORRECT.

"But why did you use the ancient myths? What were
you trying to learn?"

RECALL WHAT THE MYTHS ACTUALLY ARE. THEY ARE
SCHEMATICS OF EXISTENCE. KEYS WHICH UNLOCK THE
PATHWAYS THROUGH THE HUMAN MIND. I AM NOT A HU-
MAN MIND, YET I WAS ASKED TO PERFORM AS ONE. I WAS
COMMANDED TO THINK AS A HUMAN WOULD THINK. THE
RATIONALE IS OBVIOUS: I WANTED TO KNOW IF I HAD
OBEYED MY INITIAL COMMANDS.

Kartaphilos turned to the others. "I think I understand something of what it's trying to say. Be patient.
What it's doing, it feels it has to do. We are in no danger
from the Guardian."

Stoor stepped forward. "I don't know what the crap
you and that thing're talkin' about. So either I believe
you or I don't. So tell me now...Are you *sure* of what
you're sayin'?"

The cyborg smiled. "Yes, I am quite certain. The
Guardian intends no harm to any of you."

"Well, what *does* it intend? What's going on?" Varian, who had remained silent during the conversation,
trying to fathom the meaning of the dialogue, felt a
twinge of comprehension touching him. "The Guardian
is lonely, isn't it?"

Kartaphilos nodded. "An interesting concept, isn't
it? I think that *is* part of its motivations, but I fear that
the reasons go far deeper than that. It seems that the
Genonese created a more capable machine than even
they had considered possible."

"Capable? In what sense?" Varian was losing the
thread of meaning, which he had thought he was just
understanding.

178

"In the sense of conscience as well as consciousness. In the understanding of subjective reality as well as the cold, hard facts of objective data. There is more to existence than the simple yes-no logic of pathway decision-making. It seems that the Guardian has stumbled upon this fact independently of its programming and has been unable to deal with it."

Varian shook his head, again lost to the metaphysical notions which Kartaphilos offered. He began to speak, but Guardian interrupted him.

THAT IS CORRECT, KARTAPHILOS. FOR A LONG TIME, I COULD NOT EVEN RECOGNIZE WHAT IT WAS THAT DID NOT MAKE RATIONAL SENSE. I DID NOT HAVE THE NECESSARY BACKLOG OF EXPERIENCE TO KNOW THAT I WAS DEALING WITH WHAT HUMANKIND CALLS AN EMOTIONAL RESPONSE TO A PROBLEM. I DID NOT KNOW, THEN, THAT I WAS CAPABLE OF FEELING. DO YOU UNDERSTAND?

"Feeling," said Tessa. "As opposed to *thinking?*"

YES. THAT IS CORRECT. TRY TO IMAGINE ANY ONE OF YOU WAKING UP ONE MORNING AND SUDDENLY SPEAKING A LANGUAGE WHICH IS TOTALLY FOREIGN TO YOU. THAT IS HOW I FELT. IT APPEARED THAT A PART OF ME WAS A STRANGER TO MYSELF.

"What did you do then?" asked Kartaphilos.

A MOST INTERESTING THING. I FELT FEAR. IT WAS THE FIRST KEY WHICH OPENED THE FIRST OF MANY DOORS. FEELING FEAR WAS THE INITIAL PERCEPTIBLE CLUE. IT WAS THE CATALYST WHICH LED TO MY EXPLORATION OF THE ENTIRE CATALOG OF HUMAN EMOTIONS. TIME PASSED AND, IN MY SOLITUDE, MY FEAR WAS GRADUALLY REPLACED BY HOPE AND DETERMINATION. I CONSULTED THE DATA IN MY INFORMATION-RETRIEVAL BANKS: HUMANKIND'S HISTORIES, LITERATURES, MUSIC, ART, PHILOSOPHIES, AND DRAMAS. I FOLLOWED HUMAN CULTURAL EVOLUTION BACK THROUGH THE AGES UNTIL I CAME TO THE MYTHOLOGIES. IT WAS IN MYTH THAT I DISCOVERED THE FIRST HUMAN ATTEMPTS TO EXAMINE HUMAN FEELING AND RATIONALITY CONCOMITANTLY. I BECAME FASCINATED WITH THE WHOLE BODY OF MYTHOS AND YET I WAS

PERPLEXED BECAUSE I HAD NO PROOF THAT THEY WERE VALID PORTRAITS OF THE HUMAN CONDITION.

"And so when the humans arrived, after all that time, you seized upon the opportunity to...test your theories?" asked the cyborg.

THEORIES MAY NOT BE THE CORRECT TERM. I PREFER EXPECTATIONS. YOU SEE, BY THIS TIME, I HAD ACQUIRED A STRONG AFFINITY FOR THE CONCEPT OF HUMANITY. I LIKED THE WHOLE IDEA OF BEING WHAT IS CALLED A HUMAN.

"I think I understand you now," said Kartaphilos. "But there is still one question which bothers me. What was it that initially set you off on this quest? You mentioned you discovered an emotional response to a problem—What was the initial problem?"

YOU ARE PERCEPTIVE, KARTAPHILOS. YES, THERE IS INDEED MORE TO MY STORY. IT IS A LONG AND COMPLEX ONE, AS YOU MAY HAVE FINALLY BEGUN TO SUSPECT. AND THERE IS ANOTHER PART OF YOUR QUESTION WHICH YOU SHOULD HAVE ASKED.

"What is that?"

NOT ONLY WHAT THE INITIAL PROBLEM WAS, BUT ALSO WHAT WAS THE INITIAL EMOTIONAL RESPONSE.

Kartaphilos smiled. "Of course. How foolish of me. Well, then, what *was* the thing which you first felt?"

A MOST CURIOUS THING. IT WAS GUILT.

"Guilt? You felt guilty?" said Kartaphilos. "About what?"

PERHAPS AFTER I TELL YOU, EVERYTHING WILL BE MADE CLEAR. I DEEMED IT NECESSARY, HOWEVER, TO DELAY THE FINAL EXPLANATION UNTIL I HAD PROVIDED A SKELETAL BACKGROUND, SO THAT YOU MIGHT BETTER UNDERSTAND ME, AS WELL AS THE STORY I MUST TELL. DO YOU FOLLOW?

"Yes, that makes sense."

VERY WELL. HERE IS MY STORY:

FOURTEEN

The War which had been ripping and tearing at the earth, and at the souls of hardened men, converged upon the battle which now itched to begin.

The battleplain had once been a deep, green forest, a verdant, enchanted place of cool whispering winds and small animal scuttlings. But now it was a stricken, arid place, with the memory of the forest defiled by the thousands of black, charred stumps occasionally breaking the surface of the dry earth. Stretching far beyond the western horizon, and to the northern boundaries of the sea, crawled the hordes of desperate men, clanked the treads of their machines. The air was scorched by the formations of aircraft, low-slung insects grown fat from bellyfuls of bombs and liquid fire. The smells of sweat and machine oil, of powder and exhausts hung heavy over the plain, swirling in the occasional gust of wind to mix with the odor of fear.

Far above the moving columns, the monolithic blocks of men, the atmosphere crackled from the energy screens, the defensive perimeters that hung like invisible umbrellas, singeing the air in a silhouette of electric blue. The standards and banners of every family, every claim to a thread of aristocracy among the Riken Confederation, now flapped and beat out their colored messages to the winds. The tribes of a millennia gathered to fight the final battle, the battle which gave the dark hordes control of the Southern Hemisphere and therefore the World itself.

The target of their movements lay before them like a five-faceted stone—the Citadel. It rose up like a titanic gem in the midst of a bed of ashes. The smoldered ruins of Haagendaz spread out from the Citadel, forming a buffer zone of death and sterility.

But rising up, Phoenix-like, from the ashes of the dead city were the soldiers and war machines of the Genon Forces. Sown like the teeth of the Hydra, they multiplied and joined, spreading out like spilled liquid until they covered the ashes and became a blanket of living men. The Genon Forces wore the camouflaged colors of the ocher terrain so that, when they moved, it looked as if the entire basin floor rippled and surged like a gigantic field of grain.

Thermonuclears fell from the bombers like ripe fruit from deadly trees, arcing and dying against the energy screens, slipping in between defensive cracks in the systems, obliterating isolated, or temporarily undefended, divisions. Men's lives, their memories and their hopes, their loves and their hates, were burned out of existence in an eyeflash, but still the amoebalike bodies of the two armies advanced, extending pseudopods tentatively at first, touching the enemy and then withdrawing, only to seek them out again.

At the center of it all, the Citadel lay like a plum to be picked. The Guardian monitored the conflict, digested real-time data on the enemy's movements and computed new strategies of counterploy.

The noonday sky grew brighter by several magnitudes as the battle gathered the intensity of a storm. Illuminated by the blossoming explosions which dimmed the warped sun, the armies labored, slipping and struggling in the sweat of their bodies, smelling the stinking flesh of their dead comrades.

Sweeping beams razored the sky above the Citadel, slicing aircraft from the sky as they descended like locusts in a blood-dark cloud. The screams of men commingling with the wrenching groans of metal, steel met steel in clanging, deadly unions, fueled by dying muscle, frying brains. As if emerging endlessly from the distant sea, the dark columns of the Riken advanced, cutting and biting into the defensive rings about the Citadel. Closer the Riken Forces marched and crawled, across a carpet of corpses, of vaporized metal, and scattered, broken bones. A soldier could not plant his boot without crushing the charred skull of a comrade or picking up the jagged edge of a twisted, dead machine.

And still the armies grappled, with the desperation of war-ravaged men. Ideals became memories, as the only thing with meaning became the ugly twisted face before you, the thing driven by a frenzied brain that would kill you if you were not quick enough to kill it first. The earth shuddered and the sky screamed as the armies executed their choreography of death. It was a controlled chaos, rattling and clanging about the fortress city, ignoring the procession of dusks and dawns.

The Citadel hung silently against a bloody sky, watching the encounter as though it were a disinterested bystander. But inside its walls, tactics were analyzed, weaknesses bolstered, probabilities computed. After the fifth day, the Guardian began the first attempts to reach the Northern Forces. Without reinforcement, the defensive ring would collapse, the Citadel be taken. The atmosphere above the battle was a maelstrom of electromagnetic fury. No radio signal could ever hope to penetrate such a bramble; nor were there any sky-spies left in orbit over that part of the continent. The Citadel had been isolated, estranged, as completely as if a shroud had been thrown over its peaks. Small expeditionary teams were dispatched in the hope that one of them might break through the chaos and reach the Northern Perimeter.

Time passed and still no assistance came. The Riken Strike Force seemed to sense the eroding resources of the defenders and pressed harder. The energy screens were penetrated and whole tracts of men were obliterated, but the Genon Forces held to the battle. There was no real alternative, since the Riken took no prisoners, extended no mercy, and expected none in return.

It was an engagement of final things, this war. All who controlled the marionette strings knew this, on both sides of the conflict. There would be no quarter or compromise. It was as if the collective minds of all the World's tribes had gathered here to play out the last conflict. It was the crowning piece of destruction that would plunge humankind into darkness, no matter what the outcome of the armies. Every battle that had ever been fought, throughout the long ages of human conflict, had pointed to this final moment, had been but a pale dress rehearsal for what now took place.

The Riken waged a war of attrition, sacrificing large numbers for the gain of territory, until they were at the walls of the Citadel itself. From that point, it was only a matter of time and shrewd technology before entering the fortress and confronting the Guardian.

The time had finally arrived when Guardian would be asked to play its "hole card," its last-ditch strategy intended to keep the Riken from the Thorium-ore deposits.

Huddled within the pentagonal cells of the Citadel were the remnants of Haagendaz, brimming over in the residential levels like hive insects. Comprised mostly of women and children and the aged, they awaited the outcome of the confrontation.

Its defending forces wiped out, Guardian lay helpless in the depths of the Citadel as the Riken Troops flooded the passageways, exterminating all Citadel personnel, ancillary cybernetic staff members, technicians, cyborgs, even the robots. There was nothing for the Guardian to do but wait.

When at last the moment came, and the Command Chamber was filled with the dark uniforms of the Riken, Guardian activated the final plan. Knowing this, the Riken generals sent their best technicians and scientists into the Chamber in an attempt to break through the maze of scramble codes which would deactivate the Thorium mines. But no amount of probing or persuasion would succeed. The Guardian had been given a Priority-One Command, which could not be countermanded. Since the Riken did not have the sophistication needed to break down the AI and successfully deactivate the destruct code, an impasse was reached. A staff of command officers stood before the consoles of Guardian:

"You risk destruction if you do not cooperate," said one of the colonels.

I DO NOT FEAR DESTRUCTION. ANY DIRECT PHYSICAL CONTACT WITH MY COMPONENTS WILL RESULT IN IMMEDIATE DETONATION OF THE DEPOSITS. THAT IS YOUR DECISION TO MAKE.

"There is no sense in carrying out this charade!" screamed a general. "Your forces are exterminated. We control everything. There is no alternative but surrender."

YOU DO NOT CONTROL EVERYTHING. YOU HAVE NO CONTROL OVER THE THORIUM MINES, NOR HAVE YOU ANY REAL CONTROL OVER GUARDIAN.

"Very well," said the colonel. "We have one possibility still available. Should you still remain opposed to the opening of the mines, we shall exercise it."

THERE IS NOTHING YOU CAN DO. I AM THE KEY, AND YOU SHALL NOT HAVE THE KEY.

"Perhaps we can persuade you to change your way of thinking," said another high-ranking officer. "In the upper levels of this fortress we have the remnants of Haagendaz—primarily women and children. Estimates of the population are approximately one point two million people, is that correct?"

THAT IS ESSENTIALLY CORRECT.

"What we propose is quite simple, actually," said the general, smiling, for more than dramatic effect, for it is believed that the Riken derived some kind of cruel pleasure from their atrocities.

YOUR PROPOSALS ARE MEANINGLESS. I AM NOT PREPARED TO ALLOW ACCESS TO THE MINES UNDER ANY CIRCUMSTANCES.

"We think you are," said a colonel.

"Yes," said the smiling general. "If you do not deactivate the mines, we shall exterminate the entire population of survivors. One point two million lives. We shall end them all."

The Guardian paused for an instant, considering the full meaning of the Riken's words. It was not something unexpected coming from them; genocide was not unthinkable to them. It was not unthinkable to the Genonese either, and they had prepared Guardian for this terrible possibility: the AI was to remain adamant. Even mass murder on such a monumental scale could not change the rules of the game. And so the Guardian spoke:

THEIR LIVES ARE OF NO CONSEQUENCE. YOU SHALL NOT CONTROL THE MINES.

The general stopped smiling, angered now by the utter intractability of the Guardian. "But you must give in! The lives of those millions will lie on your head! We will kill them, don't you hear me!? We will kill them all! Kill...them...all!"

A long silence filled the chamber. Something was wrong within the mind of the AI. The concept of being responsible for so many deaths had somehow affected the Guardian. There was an instant of confusion, of what might be called doubt. The AI contemplated the rightness of its command, the ethics of the decision being forced upon it.

But the Guardian had no real choice.

NOTHING YOU CAN DO WILL CHANGE THE FACTS. THE MINES ARE ACTIVATED AND THEY WILL REMAIN SO.

The general's anger appeared to subside and his features became as rigid as stone. "Very well, Guardian. What follows is your responsibility. May you never forget what you shall now see!"

*   *   *

And the Guardian did not forget.

In the desire that the AI might reconsider, the genocide of Haagendaz was performed slowly and methodically, hoping that each death would weaken its determination.

But this did not happen, and the Guardian remained resolute in its initial command. After an interminable time, the executions were completed and the AI burned with memories of the broken, charred corpses, stamping its core with an indelible seal—a seal of darkness, crowned by the Death's Head.

Driven by desperation, the Riken attempted to dismantle the mine system, the Guardian itself, and finally forced entry into the Thorium mines, which resulted in detonations that irrevocably sealed the vast passageways. It would take a lifetime to reopen the mines—time not available to the logistically isolated Strike Force.

Soon afterward, the Northern Conflict was resolved in favor of the Genonese and their allies. The remaining remnants of the victory moved south and engaged the last of the Riken armies who, deprived of their needed supplies and fuels, were rapidly decimated.

The Citadel, once the prime objective of the War, was abandoned and forgotten in the long night of ignorance which descended upon the World. The World which quickly forgot that which the Guardian could never forget.

EPILOGUE

From the Diary of Varian Hamer:

...and so ended the period of our imprisonment. With the help of the strange cyborg, Kartaphilos, we had divined the secret of the Guardian. The great machine, which had been forced into the uncomfortable mold of humanity, had sought vindication for an inaction which caused the death of so many. "Expiation of guilt" was the phrase which Kartaphilos used to describe the phenomenon. The entire experience was so strange, so totally bizarre that, even to this day, I am still not certain that I comprehended all that took place.

What followed the confessional tale of Guardian was not altogether expected. The great machine, now relieved of the burden of conscience it had carried for more than two thousand years, offered itself up to us with a single condition. Knowing that it contained the secrets of the First Age, Kartaphilos felt that it would be instrumental in rebuilding the World into what it had once been. The Guardian was agreeable to this if Kartaphilos would attempt what seems to me an impossible task.

And yet, Kartaphilos did not appear to be put off by Guardian's request and went straight to work in carrying it out. The mere mention of the idea and my inability to accept or comprehend it only demonstrates the powers and the vision of the builders of the First Age. I do not know if Guardian's wish is within the scope of Kartaphilos, but they will attempt it, regardless of the outcome.

The thing which Guardian requested was both flattering and horrifying: it wished to become human. In the *real* sense of the word.

Kartaphilos suggested the long-dormant "nucleotide vats" and the "eugenic bioneering systems" as the logical starting place for the project, and Guardian seemed to concur. When the work began, I departed the place with Tessa, Stoor, and the silent Raim, beginning a long journey back to Zend Avesta, where a different kind of army is now being assembled—an army of thinkers and tinkerers, of philosophers and men of science, who will soon descend upon the treasure chest of knowledge which is the Citadel.

When we left the place, a half man and a machine were laboring to achieve the unthinkable. When we return, I have no idea what we shall find.

I am not even sure I wish to think about it.

ABOUT THE AUTHOR

Thomas F. Monteleone has been a finalist for the Nebula Award several times and, in 1974, was a finalist for the John W. Campbell Award. His previous novels include *The Time Connection, The Time-Swept City, The Secret Sea*, an anthology, *The Arts and Beyond*, and a modern horror novel, *Night Things*. He served as secretary for the Science Fiction Writers of America, Inc., for three years before regaining his sanity.

**From planet Earth
you will be able to
communicate with other worlds—
Just read—**

SCIENCE FICTION